6/24/19

Cosecha
and Other Stories

By Aurora Levins Morales
and Rosario Morales

Palabrera Press
Cambridge, Massachusetts
@2014 Aurora Levins Morales

Cover design by Aurora Levins Morales

Cover photo of Rosario Morales, pregnant with Aurora Levins Morales,
1953, from Levins Morales family collection.

Book design by Design Action
1710 Franklin Street #300
Oakland, CA 94612
Tel. 510.452.1912
info@designaction.org

ISBN 978-0983683117
Library of Congress Control Number: 2013922854

"A Remedy for Heartburn" first appeared in *Ms Magazine*, "Tsu Gott Vel
Ikh Veynen" in *Bridges: A Journal for Jewish Feminists and Our Friends*,
"Vivir Para Ti" in *The American Voice*, "Dulce de Naranja" in *Las Christmas:
Favorite Latino Authors Share Their Holiday Memories* (Knopf, 1998) and
"chicken house goat girls" in *Yellow Medicine Review*.

para las nietas y los nietos
Nico, Emilio, Manuel, Alicia, Olivia

Thanks to my father, Richard Levins, for his support: material, intellectual, political and emotional.

Many people helped me navigate this process of grieving and creativity: my brothers Ricardo and Alejandro, my daughter Alicia and niece Olivia, my honorary sisters Freda Hauser and Ruth Mahaney, the rabbis, service leaders, and congregation of Kehilla Community Synagogue, the staff and participants of the "grief camp" offered by the Bay Area Jewish Healing Center, my dear friends Patty Berne and Chela Blitt, and Becky Logan, also most dear, whom I also now grieve.

Special thanks for many kinds of care, inspiration and help to Abram Ojure, Arielle Rosenberg, Brittany Rode, Caitlin Churchill, Catalina Bartlett, Cathy Hoffman, Cherie Brown, Denny Bergman, Donna Collantino, Glen Rothfeld, Gwyn Kirk, Ilana Lerman, Joanna Ware, Jonah Daniel, Joshua Muscat, Leora Abelson, Lissy Romanow, Lorenzo García, Marcie Rendon, María Judith Colón, Mónica Gomery, Rachel Andelman, Ray-Ray Farrales, Ricardo Levins Morales, Shannon Custer.

My co-counselors: Alya Davidman, Catalina Bartlett, Glenn Hauer, Isha Mckenzie-Mavinga, Joelle Hochman, Julie Saxe-Taller, Maria Judith Colón, Michael Saxe-Taller.

Table of Contents

Before Words

This book is full of stories of death. It was not intentional. They were written in widely scattered moments, over many years. But when we decided to make another book, this was what was in the basket, long before my mother's cancer made it achingly relevant.

And because she had written *Y tuesta el sol* about her parents' deaths, because we spent so many decades in conversation, because I accompanied her through her own dying, was there at her last breath, washed her body, dressed her, placed her inside the basket woven of banana leaves, in her shroud of golden silk, because in spite of so much that was beyond her control, she owned her dying, I wanted to write the response to my mother's call, the companion piece, my own telling of her death.

But I can't do it. I'm not ready, and this book is. The loss of her is still too vast and disorderly within me. I have vivid scraps, but they don't make a pattern. There's no quilt. Parts of the fabric are missing, the necessary balance of color and texture that would make it whole. I can't force my telling. It's not some winter crocus, to be pushed into unseasonal bloom.

Trust yourself, my mother says, as talkative in death as she was in life. Most of the time I feel her airborne, perched outside my window, or floating through the room, commenting inside my head, but today I have been imagining her under the ground, lying on the earth in her red dress, shrugging a little, saying *It'll happen when it happens.*

I keep resisting saying this is our final collaboration. I think there's more to do, more of her words to weave together with mine, so I won't say that. Instead, I say, this is the book that we began before her death, and I finished afterwards, alone. This is the harvest of what we did together. Come to the table, she would say. Eat, dears, eat.

Aurora Levins Morales

December, 2013

A Remedy For Heartburn

In Memory of Doña Gina Torres of Bartolo

Our people have always been good at digesting even the most indigestible items on life's menu. Insults that would give a conquistador a heart attack—we have learned to wipe them off our faces and put the handkerchief away for later consideration. Sometimes our pockets bulge with insults, and personally, I have a little red leather coin purse that I had to quit using because it wouldn't close anymore. There were so many insults and so few coins that I was always turning up something nasty whenever I dug around for a subway token. When you run out of storage space, sometimes a hiss or sneer or some offhand and cheerful piece of disrespect goes down your throat and your stomach has to deal with it. It's not easy. It gives you heartburn like you wouldn't believe, but we can do it. All of us are experts.

As for this jaw-breaking language that gets pushed into our mouths every time we ask for a piece of bread, we're the best there is at digesting that. We roll it around in our sweet tropical saliva and spit it back, sweeter and sharper and altogether more sabroso. Everything they dish out to us, we soften and satirize with our acrobatic tongues. We wash with Palmolíveh and brush with super-white Colgátch. We rub Vicks Vaporú on our chests when we get a cold, and halfway through each day of hard work and boredom, we stop and have some lonche. Not at home on weekends. We never have lonche at home. But weekdays when we step into some hallway with a counter and six red stools and order a sánguich—that's lonche.

That's hard to digest, too—tasteless white bread, a smear of mayonnaise, a few wrinkled slices of ham or old-shoe beef, a square of what these people were actually not embarrassed to call American cheese and some kind of a pale green leaf. But our people have hard stomachs. Hunger makes people more like goats. I've known old men who lived for months on end on nothing but the malanga they dug out of other people's land. The USDA surplus lunches they served at our grade school comedor were excellent training for the immigrant eater's lonche break. The kids used to say the beans tasted of cucaracha, they'd been sitting in some warehouse so long. As for the lukewarm powdered milk we gagged on, it was what each of us was told to be grateful for—it would make us strong and healthy—and, if we got good grades and had respect for our elders, it would make us worthy of our citizenship in that great nation los Estados Unidos, where everything good came from.

At home, there was a lot to swallow, too. The men swallowed the bad price of coffee and pocket size bottles of rum and the women swallowed hunger and fear for their children, and the mean language and hard hands of their drunk husbands. There was boredom enough to make you go crazy looking for something to gossip about. Petty feuds between hard-up people who had to find someplace to put all the grief and desperation of watching poverty carve furrows in their lives as deep as the rains did in the hillsides. If you lacked the staying power for neighborly backbiting, you could join a religion, one of those fervent, severe, evangelical sects that were always holy rolling through the mountains in search of depressed and lonely people ready to try anything. Or you could drown yourself in illicit love affairs and star in your own novela, playing hourly in the patios and kitchens of your scandalized vecinas. Or if you were lucky, you had the gift of humor and could laugh hard and long at each of the slaps and cocotazos life dealt you.

I said before that hunger makes people more like goats, able to swallow tin cans and get something like nourishment from them. But sometimes hunger makes people fierce, like those wild dogs, left to starve by the humans, that go hunting in packs, stealing chickens and small pets and sometimes mauling people. Every so often, when they all band together, they do manage to maul some people. That kind of anger was hard to lay hands on where I grew up. Discouragement left us numb.

My mother said I was a very hungry child, always wanting more, which there wasn't much of because Papi would usually take his pay to the store and drink a few palitos and a few more, before he turned the leftovers over to Mami. Then he would stay up all night giving crazy orders, like no-one could sleep as long as he was awake. He would play the TV and the radio at the same time, and turn on all the lights, and go from room to room, banging pots together and dragging us out of bed to keep him company in his drunkard's nightmare. The rest of the time, when he was sober, he was a sweet enough guy, affectionate and funny. But as for me, I was always hungry and bad tempered.

Not Mami. At least not that anyone could tell. Everyone called her a saint. You know that way that Puerto Rican country women can look at a woman's suffering and turn it into a kind of special attention from God? My mother was that kind of a saint. She worked twice as hard as Papi, in the house and on the farm; longer and harder than anyone else I knew. Her house was ramshackle, but spotless, her food was exquisite, her garden plot was in order and she always knew where a sweet orange tree was ready for picking, or a bunch of the best cooking bananas had gotten big enough to cut. She was the one everyone came and asked for twigs of oregano and bits of geranium to plant. She was good humored and generous, and several times a month my father threw her and all of us kids out of doors, tore up her meager belongings, raged and cursed at her, and hit her a few clumsy blows across the back and shoulders. Although she yelled at him to leave the kids alone, she never complained about his treatment of her. So they called her a saint.

The only thing to my knowledge that she actually longed for was a good house with a nice kitchen. But every day of her life she contrived and conspired for her children, and especially for me, her ravenous little goat. She saw to it that I stayed in high school by doing the extra work I would have done, and she picked coffee for don Luis three years in a row to send me to secretarial school in the city. I stayed with a cousin of hers who gave me room and board for helping out with the house and kids, and learned to type and answer telephones, and memorize all the correct formats for business letters.

I got a job in an office, with some nice people, and at first having even that small salary belong to me, in my own name, was enough to please me. After a while, seeing how little it really could buy made it less of a thrill, but sending some of it home to Mami, secretly, so Papi couldn't turn it into Palo Viejo, was satisfying.

After a couple of years I met Papo, and in not too long I married him and we went back to New York, where he'd been working the year before. He was a good dancer and a hard worker, and had to be because it turned out he was keeping three separate families of his own. One of them was a woman with two kids, who lived in the Bronx. She was under the impression that he'd been visiting a sick mother on the island and at the very moment that Doña Justa was kicking up her heels at my wedding, this woman, Sara, was lighting candles for her preservation from some kind of kidney disease. The other was Cindy, (her mother had named her Lucinda), an eighteen year old he started in on about six months after we moved into our place in Brooklyn. By the time I found out about her she was very pregnant. She also lived only a block away from us, which was convenient for him. As soon as I had some steady work, I left him to his other families and moved in with my cousin Tinita. I had never actually mentioned to Papo that a little outpatient surgery I'd had done a few years back had insured that I would not end up like Cindy or Sara. Then again, he had never asked.

Well, about then I signed up for a class at City College. This girl-friend of mine at my job, Julia, told me about it. It was a class about history, our history. The man who taught it was smart. Puerto Rican, but brought up in los Nueva Yores. I love that expression. It's one of the ways we take something too big to swallow—a country as big as a continent, and all full of americanos—and make it bite size. New York is about the limit of what we want to think about, so we wave a vague hand north, south and west of it and call it all los Nueva Yores. I think this fellow grew up in Chicago.

Anyway we learned all about the Conquistadores and the Taínos and the African slaves. We learned about the Spanish governors who ran Puerto Rico like a boot camp, and about Betances and his buddies trying to get a fight going to kick them out, and then the way the US just helped themselves when Spain got old and weak and tired. Ricardo, that's our teacher, told us about the big strikes they had for better work and pay, and about this woman who went around reading speeches to the tobacco workers while the bosses thought she was reading them novels, and writing her own magazine called <u>La Mujer</u> where she said that marriage was nothing but a pain and women should love whoever they wanted without any scandal, and leave them when they were ready to, without any fuss. I thought about that for a long time, and I finally told Julia maybe she wore boots and smoked cigars, but this Luisa Capetillo was right about one thing anyway. Marriage had not been set up for the benefit of any woman I had ever heard of. Taking this class was making me very hungry indeed. Not goat hungry. The wild dog kind. The kind where you only swallow what tastes good to you and spit the rest out, snarling.

I thought about Mami's life. I had been expecting for years to hear that Papi had driven the jeep over a cliff on his way home from the store, but by some kind of a miracle, Papi had suddenly decided not to drink anymore. He had given the old house to my brother Paquito and his family, and had finally built Mami the house she always wanted. It was made of cement, with nothing a termite might fancy to eat. The rain stayed out, and so did the rats. It had a real kitchen with a Kenmore stove and a Whirlpool refrigerator. It even had a water heater, and with fifteen or twenty minutes notice, it was possible to have a hot shower, something my mother had never had before in her long life of cold water bucket baths at noon.

Then one day I got a letter from Paquito's wife, Migdalia. Mami had been saying lately that food just didn't agree with her. "You know how Mamá is—she never complains." But finally she had mentioned that her stomach hurt, and one day Migdalia found her vomiting. They took her to the doctor in Ponce, and the whole way she kept telling them it was silly, she just had a flu—it was from the cold weather lately. But when they took some pictures it turned out she had so much cancer in her stomach that nothing else fit. They said they had to operate immediately, then, when they had her open, they decided not to bother because there wasn't any good stomach left. So they sewed her up and sent her home with some pain pills, and three days later she died.

Now cancer isn't something that happens overnight. It must have been secretly growing in her, a thwarted appetite for flesh, for a long time. I've been sitting here thinking and I believe it was hunger that killed Mami. Not the times there wasn't enough to eat, because

Mami always found ways to stretch a little bacalao a long way. I think it was the wild dog hunger in her that never had anything to feed on but the insults she swallowed, and those English brand names all full of corners, and the vicious retorts she never made to my father's abuse. Migdalia says they offered to drive to the farmácia and call me, but she wouldn't let them. She didn't send any special message, no last words for me, but I've been piecing together the clues.

The kind of hunger that ate Mami's stomach can't be kept in. It isn't house-broken, tame. It can go years looking like a farm animal, hauling water, carrying wood, cooking and digging and trying to stretch a handful of change into a living. It can even be hit with a stick and cursed for its lameness, but watch out. Sooner or later it gnaws at the rope that binds it, and if that rope is your own life, you die. That's the message she sent me. Her hungriest daughter. The one she managed to send away. I imagine her showing me her cancer-eaten belly, holding up the tumors the way she used to show me the yautía she pulled out of the ground. If you swallow bitterness, she says, you eat death.

Recently I don't eat death anymore, and I've been doing my piece to change the national diet of Puerto Rico. Death al escabeche, death al fricasé, death frito and death con habichuelas. I've learned a lot of history by now, and I know that at least since Colón, we've always been hungry and dying. Some of us have gotten fierce enough to attack the ones who starve us, but mostly the wild dog kind just maul their neighbors and themselves. And the rest of us, we're good farm animals. We get milked all our lives, and then butchered for soup.

Instead of swallowing bitterness, I've been spitting it up. In a way it was Luisa Capetillo who gave me the idea. I got home from Mami's funeral and that Monday after work I began this book. Now it's done. It's a kind of cookbook I wrote for Mami. A different set of recipes than the ones she lived her life by, those poisonous brews of resignation and regret, those soups of monotony and neighborly malice that only give you gas. Each recipe has a piece of what she gave me though, nourishing as ñame, floating in a rich broth. It starts this way. *My mother taught me to cook. The name of the first dish was dutiful daughter, but she had a special way with it, so it turned out different from what her neighbors made.* There are recipes for Amores a la Capetillo (subtitled "for Papo"), and a Medianoche full of all my mother never screamed at my father. There's one called Secretarial Lonche that calls for a good stiff pinch of union wage. But my favorite recipe is the one at the very end. Remedy For Heartburn. *This is the most challenging recipe in my book, comadres. The ingredients? You already have them. In your pockets, in your purses, in your bellies and your bedrooms. For this kind of broth, there can't be too many cooks. Get together. Stir the stuff around. Listen to your hunger. Get ready. Get organized.*

Tsu Got Vel Ikh Veynen

Tsu got del ikh veynen
Mit a groys geveyn
Tsu vos bin ikh geboyren
A neyterin tsu zein?
To God I cry out
with a great cry,
Why was I born
To be a seamstress?

—Davis Edelstadt

1

Six years at Melody Bra and Girdle Company, sewing corsets and girdles. Another year at the Donel Foundation until it folded. Four years at Imperial Brassiere Corporation, traveling two hours each way, working the three-stitch machine for ninety-five dollars a week. This is the work history on a job application of my grandmother's that my mother found in a drawer, dating from sometime in the early sixties.

Women in Puerto Rico had been doing home-based needlework for garment companies since the beginning of the century, and especially after the start of World War I, when supplies of embroidered work from Europe were cut off, leaving the department stores high and dry. By the 1930s, sewing was Puerto Rico's second largest industry, but it was hidden away in women's homes, so economists and historians called it "marginal." In 1921, when my great-grandfather

Don Ramón Morales died of pernicious anemia in his forties, and left his wife Doña Rosario with a property in Naranjito, and twelve children to raise, there was nothing marginal about it. The older boys worked the tobacco and pasture land, and Doña Rosario turned the big Morales family house into a garment workshop, attaching piles of bodices to skirts to make nurses' uniforms, and turning out miles of lace tablecloths, acres of embroidery, every kind of fancy-work she and her young daughters-in-law could contrive.

In the 1950s, when my parents moved to the remote mountain community of Indiera Baja, women still traveled down to Yauco and Maricao to pick up handkerchiefs and pre-cut pieces of blouses and shirts and dresses, which they took home to sew and embroider, and then exchanged for new sleeves and collars and handkerchiefs, and a thin sheaf of dollars. It was one of the few ways rural women could get their hands on cash. The men went in and out of the infernos of the cane fields and spent half the year sharpening their machetes for the next harvest, or anxiously watched the sky, waiting to see if drought would shrivel the coffee blossoms, storms strip the branches, or the sun fail to ripen the berries. But women plied their needles in every season, rain or sun, at any time of day or night, while they kept an eye on the children, the boiling pot of beans, the hungry chickens scratching in the yard, and the family plot full of bananas, malanga, and gandules.

For my grandmother's generation of migrants, it was still the best option. You could wash clothes for a hospital or a laundry company—my grandmother did that, too—or be a maid. Or you could sew. Garment work, piece work, at the minimum wage. Her longest stint at one place was at Melody Bra and Girdle, between 1950 and 1956. It was the flood period of Puerto Rican migration. Thousands of women who had being doing piecework in their wooden houses in the countryside of the island, poured into the sweatshops of the

New York garment industry. They sat at rows of noisy machines, doing the same thing over and over and over, needle points flashing a fraction of an inch from their fingers. *Feather stitch machine. Three stitch machine.* The needles whirr, pierce the fabric, rip along seams with a deafening clatter. As each piece is finished, it's tossed into bin. No time to glance at it. The next one is already pushing under the devouring food, guided by their hands.

During those same years that my grandmother, Lola Morales by nickname and marriage, fed millions of elastic undergarments through her machine, Lolita Lebron was also working in the New York City garment trade. How much did that harsh labor intensify her patriotic fury? In 1954 she led three men of the Nationalist Party in a guerrilla action against the U.S. congress. The intent was not assassination. On the floor of the chamber, pompous men were attempting to ensure that the United Nations did not meddle with their colony, by declaring in tones of outraged sovereignty that Puerto Rico's affairs were purely internal and nobody's business. In that deafening silence in which her life and the lives of all the people she knew and loved were casually erased, Lolita and her companions fired guns into the air and unfurled the flag of their nationhood, as proof that we did, in fact, exist. I say "we" because six days earlier, I had been born into that same dispossession. Lolita and her three companions spent the next twenty-five years in prison for that outcry, while the needles continued to rise and fall over the hands of her sisters and cousins and nieces and neighbors.

My grandmother hated it. Even her irrepressible urge to laugh became muted there. She hated the pressure of keeping up to speed, doing the same deadly work over and over at breakneck pace. She hated the displaced hostility of the women, screaming their frustrations at each other, their anger erupting into slaps and curses. She hated the danger. Once, preoccupied with her troubled and troubling younger daughter, her hand was caught in the machine, and a needle went all the way through her finger. I imagine her pinned there, struggling for flight, like one of those tropical butterflies with pollen dusted wings whose labor brings blossom to fruit, trapped for some collector's use. She hated the danger and the long commutes and the low pay, and the insulting attitudes of the bosses, and she went on hating it for twenty years.

2

The needles break, fifteen a minute
and from my fingers the blood spurts out.
To God I cry out, with a great cry,
Why was I born to be a seamstress?

Those words were written by David Edelstadt, a Jewish poet of the New York garment sweatshops of an earlier generation of underpaid and exploited pieceworkers. Workers like my great-grandmother Leah Shevelev and her little sister Betty, once Rivieka. Betty was in her early teens when she arrived from a country village in the Ukraine and went into the shops to sew for ten hours or more a day.

I've hardly fallen asleep before I wake again
And with my tired bones,
I drag myself back to work…
Mit meine kranke beyner.

Workers like my step-grandpa Abe's sister, who died in the Triangle Shirtwaist fire. The Triangle Shirtwaist company locked their employees into an upper room. Presumably so they wouldn't slip away early. Presumably to extract the last penny's worth of value from them before they were released, limp with exhaustion, at the end of the day. When the building caught fire, they burned among the shirtwaists, or leapt to their deaths in the street below. *Tsu got vel ikh veynen, mit a groys geveyn, tzo vos bin ikh geboyren a neyterin tsu zein?*

Men also worked in the needle trades. For years my great-grandfather Abe lived in Bridgeport, Connecticut during the week, and came home to see his family in Brooklyn on weekends. He was a foreman at a factory that made nurses' uniforms, and so received enough pay to make the weekly trip. The workers under him didn't. They lived in boardinghouses and sent their paychecks home without the gift of seeing their loved ones' faces, smelling their skin, touching their hands.

At one time, during the early years, he was also foreman of a small shop where Leah and Betty worked. The story is that the women went out on strike against the management he represented. It would certainly have been in their character. They were women not easily intimidated by authority. In a 1931 article, written for the unemployed women's circle she led, my great-grandmother wrote about her own grandmother, the one who "instilled the revolutionary spark in me." She was a rabbi's wife, and lived in the city of Kremenchug, on the Dnieper River. The *rebbetsin* was highly respected, the local arbiter of disputes, and a better scholar than her husband, but Jewish law proclaimed she could not become a rabbi herself. "This is God's law," the men told her. So she stood up in *shul*, said "Your God is a man," and walked out, taking her husband with her. The oldest family photograph I have is of her daughter Henke, and the most striking things I see there are her steady gaze, and the way her hands, at rest in her lap, look just like mine.

3

I learned to sew from my mother, on an old treadle Singer sewing machine., set up in the hallway of our house in Indiera Baja. Although both my mother's grandmothers were skilled needlewomen, my mother grew up Harlem and the Bronx, separated from that tradition. There must have been a sewing machine, because she remembers riding the pedal, but her mother had no interest in voluntary sewing, and more than enough of the compulsory kind. What clothing they had, they bought.

Instead, my mother learned to sew in the public schools of New York in the 1930s and 1940s. She loved physics and theater and literature. She loved learning with a passionate hunger, as she loved whatever took her away from the airless, violent pressure cooker at home. In school they knitted socks for soldiers, and she learned to embroider, read patterns, and assemble garments with a marvelous stitch, half running half backstitch, the fastest and easiest for hand sewing long seams, which she taught me as a child—"See, the backstitch anchors, the running stitch flies!"

Today that love of craft and color has made my mother a quilter. Her walls dazzle the eye with original, brilliantly colored creations, full of tropical foliage and lizards, sun and visible wind. She took the needle from her mother's tired hands and made it sing. These are not the incongruous yoyo quilts of my childhood and hers, a net of squashed cloth bags, stitched together at the edges: lacy, delicate and useless, made only to drape over things and satisfy the Puerto Rican passion for covering up furniture with everything from doilies to fringed mats. Hers are well-stitched and solid, full of the world she sees, like the piece I saw at the Oakland Museum, by an African American woman who had embroidered the constellations as seen from her front porch, then quilted in each field of the plantation, with the lines of the plowing to show the contours of the hills. It was her view, a map of the place where she had lived her life.

For my wedding, my mother made me a wall quilt, which became the cover of our first book together. There are three horizontal panels. Each one has a small house, with a corrugated roof, shaded by banana leaves. The miracle is the light. The houses rise, one above the other—at dusk with gleaming windows, in dizzying midday blue, in the flooding yellow of a tropical morning—like a tower perched over the coastal waters, like the slums of La Perla hanging off the walls of Old San Juan, precarious and resilient, drenched in sea spray.

Along that surf washed northern coast of Puerto Rico they still make *mundillo*, a craft brought by the lace makers of southern Spain. Women sit wrapping white threads around an elaborate arrangement of pins stuck into a little pillow, then rearranging them according to a pattern. Out of the thicket of silver pins flow rivers of flowers and fans, panels of knots and bows, dense medallions and airy borders. This is the work my aunts labored at under the stern eye of their mother-in-law: tablecloths, christening gowns, wedding dresses and mantillas. This is the work my great-grandmother Leah did when she made the now fragile piece of linen, cross-stitched with Russian letters, part of the household goods she brought with her when she boarded the ship in Odessa bound for Ellis Island and the rows of sewing machines. Each minute woven square is surrounded by knotted space, a record of her days, of hours spent tying delicate threads into little bunches. For love and for bread, the women who came before me worked needle and thread.

4

When I was a child, you went to Doña Tata to have your school uniforms made up, or to Doña Luisa in town for a wedding dress or a gown for a quinceañera. But the days of neighborhood seamstresses and tailors are long over. Most of our clothing is made in the new garments districts of our country in Bangkok and Manila, in Taipei and a hundred maquiladoras strung along the Mexican border the way the old sweatshops once lined the streets of the Lower East Side. Which is not to say that the sweatshops are gone from the U.S., or even from New York. Walking along a street right here in Oakland, I got a glimpse once, through an open door, of three dozen Asian women making men's blue work shirts in a dusty, noisy room without windows. Then a white man came and closed the door in my face.

The pants I bought yesterday say on the label, Crafted with Pride in the USA. Probably in the South, I imagine the tired woman who zipped this black cotton along the presser foot of a gigantic machine, and then did another, and another, and another. The room is full of cotton dust and the roaring of machinery, and when she gets home, she's sore in every muscle. Her ears ring from the battering noise, and she coughs up threads and motes of cotton that make her chest ache. But she fixes dinner for her kids, and whoever else lives there. She does the laundry and sets out clothing for all of them to put on in the morning, and then lies in bed, wound up by the tension of boredom, with her *kranke beyner*, waiting to drag them back again in the morning. Not that much has changed.

What happened to all the bras and girdles my grandmother made? Or the shirtwaists and uniforms my great-grandparents sweated over? Most of them are probably landfill by now, all that nylon and elastic worn out by hard working women and thrown in among the rubbish heaps of the fifties. Landfill, or smoke, incinerated as rags and thrown up into the atmosphere. Maybe some of the shirts are still around, cut into patches to mend a hole in someone's pants. Used to line a pillowcase. Perhaps the unworn bits embroidered and put away in a chest for a grandchild, or placed at the pale heart of a quilt.

Or maybe it's all gone, all those threads unraveled. But thousands of people went to work each day in the garments my people made. Ladies served tea and learned to type in those shirtwaists Abe's sister died for. Nurses saved and lost lives in the uniforms my great-grandfather and his co-workers missed their families for, that my great aunts were housebound over. Generations of people were clothed and kept from cold. Women strapped themselves into undergarments that reshaped their bodies and then went out and found work that bought the beans, or stayed home and cooked the beans, or both. They went on their way, did their jobs, raised their families, told their stories. In the ordinary lives of millions of people, the work of those hands still holds.

Mundillo

Each afternoon while the bananaquits rioted in the honeysuckle vines, the women of the house gathered in the shade of the green veranda with baskets of white thread and the sharp implements of their trade, and made lace. Looking over the edge of the ship as the island fell away behind her, Delia saw how the curved wooden planks cut the green water into white froth, and raising her face into the wind, she laughed that full, rich laughter that was to stay with her when every other sense had left her, until at the age of ninety three she laughed in the face of death, alone in a dark and silent universe.

No-one else in that embroidered world shut in by the frame of the porch railing, the plaza promenade, the tiny movements of lace-making, could have imagined herself on this ship, steaming away into the north. It was one o' clock. They would be sitting there now, making their rivers of spider web, fashioning scallops and fans, spirals and zigzags, button-like flowers with splayed, delicate pet-als. It was such a restrained little dance of the hands, without hips or bellies or ankles. White threads twirled among silver pins, and the women's fingers moved through the thicket like birds. A collar for Doña Marta. A christening dress for Doña Elvira's sickly new son. Waves. Sunbursts. Little pearly knots of thread to be scat-tered like shells across Doña Rosa's hall table. But Delia dreamt of the Charleston and the Lindy Hop danced in glittering dresses, the arched back draped across strong arms, the soft click of heels flying across a polished floor.

On the other side of the deck someone was whistling a tango, full of wild and sorrowful twists and turns. *Arrabal amargo, metido en mi vida....* She had heard that song on the shiny new Victrola her brother-in-law Felipe brought back from New York for Mercedita. Doña Inez considered tangos an evil influence on young girls' minds, and the machine had lasted only two weeks before she shrouded it in doilies and it became another piece of stifled furniture in the formal dining room.

Doña Inez Vega had been blessed with twelve sons, like the twelve apostles. Franco, the eldest, managed the family's remaining acres of pasture, sugar and tobacco. The others came and went from jobs in the North. Their wives stayed in the long wooden house with the slatted shutters and wide, shaded veranda, dripping with jasmine and honeysuckle and purple trinitaria, listening to the writings of St. Teresa de Ávila which Doña Inez could recite from memory, and making the white blouses, nurses' uniforms and intricate lace that kept them dressed and fed after the untimely death of Don Florencio. White cotton sleeves set with tiny stitches into the armholes of bodices. Crisp hems on the uniforms that were packed and sent back to Philadelphia and Baltimore, and from there to hospitals and clinics in dozens of other cities and towns. White threads dancing through the maze of pins, tangling and twisting into acres of tantalizing daisies, sedate roses, bewildering spiral staircases, and scalloped edges on which the still wealthy among the lowland families set their best imported china while they hoped for better times.

Mercedita could feel the humidity in the air like a pressure on her temples. In a few hours it would become clear to everyone that Delia had not returned from her mother's house, and then the storm would burst upon them. The thread broke in her fingers and she let the frayed end trail across her hand.

"Atiende, Merce".

"Si, Doña Inez".

Nothing would have persuaded her to take such an uncertain path, to forsake the infrequent but sweet affections of Felipe, the company of her sisters by marriage, the repetitions of their daily life, even the stern vigilance of Doña Inez, for that uncharted wilderness of choices where Delia was bound.

Mercedita had been the first of the daughters-in-law to arrive, and for some time, she had born the full brunt of Doña Inez' uprightness. Merce was a naturally lively girl, from a less prominent family than the Vegas had once been, and Doña Inez had felt called upon to instruct her in the proper behavior for a young woman whose husband had taken the boat to New York. Her parents had negotiated her marriage to Felipe, who was the second son, and ten years older than her. He had wooed her with flowers and bits of ribbon and once or twice a stolen kiss, but the arrangements had been made by their families. Once married, he had made shy and silent love to her every night in the tiny bedroom that was their only privacy, and left early each morning with a kiss on her cheek, to conduct mysterious business in San Juan while she learned to wind thread and tie the miniscule knots of the family craft. Every afternoon, Felipe returned in time for a cup of coffee before the evening meal, and after lingering over the after-dinner cup, they retired early to bed. This quiet alternation of days of domestic intricacy and nights of awkward passion had continued for four weeks, then he had turned her over to his mother to be taught the skills Doña Inés deemed necessary for the wife of a Vega, while he learned the trade of a bank teller in the new hub of the island's world. At seventeen, she had been married for two years and had seen her husband for a total of twelve weeks.

She had welcomed Beatriz with enthusiasm. She was the bride of Juan Bautista, a stern, preoccupied young man to whom Mercedita had absolutely nothing to say. But Beatriz had turned out to be an unrefreshing companion. She was from what Delia later called "la alta suciedad," the exalted clay of the Buenaventuras, and believed with all her dignified soul that a gracious queenly manner was both her obligation, and her reward for ancestral virtue. She was unimaginative and smug, and while the younger girls muttered about the endless needlework, would only say in gentle reproof that to make things of beauty was a worthy occupation for a lady, and that they would all be improved by attending to Doña Inés' recitals of hypnotic verses and saintly reflections, which stretched through the long, stifling afternoons on the veranda, while the birds screamed among the vines.

It was a relief to Merce when shy Mario brought the exuberant Delia into that little world the less reverent neighbors were beginning to call "el convento," where Doña Inés decreed a strict quarter of an hour limit on the young wives' chaperoned paseos around the town plaza, and carefully scrutinized every caller.

Isabel Perea and Flavia Gonzalez had come together, married within a week of each other to Dionisio and Ignacio, the sixth and seventh of the Vega boys, who promptly, in their turn, embarked on the great migration, the one into a retail store on the Lower East Side, the other to wait tables in one of the grand hotels of New York, gleaming with crystal and gold paint. Their mother never knew that for that job, Ignacio had pretended to be Italian. Isa and Flavia were so terrified of their mother-in-law that they hardly spoke in her presence or out of it, and kept their eyes lowered, even when Delia's outrageous whispered comments made the corners of their mouths twitch nervously.

Today there was no chatter. Doña Inez did not stand for levity. Even at the sedate bingo game she allowed her daughters-in-law on Saturday afternoons, there was no laughter allowed. Only Delia had defied her with explosive little bursts of giggling that usually started Mercedita sniggering into her cupped palm. "Mercedes," Doña Inés would say in her most stately voice, "please use a handkerchief if you must sneeze."

Mi Buenos Aires queriiiido...cuahahahando te volveré a veeeeer... Delia watched the last wrinkle on the horizon sink into the water and although she didn't know it would be forty years before she saw it again, a sudden coolness of the ocean air made her wrap her shawl tighter around her shoulders.

Amidst the clattering din of the machines Delia could not hear what her friend Rosi was saying, but she had learned to read lips. The letter from Mario had found her three days ago, and Rosi, dying of curiosity, was asking for the millionth time what he had said. She laughed at Rosi and shook her head, and in the sign language all the seamstresses at the factory used, invited her to go dancing that night at their favorite Harlem club.

For three months after the day of Delia's inexplicable flight, Mario had obeyed his formidable mother's edict, and made no attempt to trace his young wife. Doña Inés was sure that Delia would be back, repentant and ready to resume. Ten days after her departure, a postcard had arrived from New York, which Mario had snatched up from the little table where Moncha the criada had deposited it, so that no one else ever read it.

"Querido Mario—I like to dance and I hate making mundillo. If you want to dance with me, ask for me at Doña Flora Pacheco's boarding house on Third Street. Your loving wife, Delia."

Each night, surrounded by the droning of crickets and the sharp exchanges of the coquis, he had lain awake worrying about her. He imagined her funny face stained with tears, sucked in by hunger, tossed and turned at the thought of her alone in the cold streets, or even worse, not alone, harassed, perhaps, by predatory men she didn't know how to resist. Finally he had gotten up one midnight, lit the kerosene lamp, and written back. After that he had slept peacefully until after dawn, and then he had gone to the city to book passage.

But tonight, walking through the streets of the Lower East Side looking for Doña Flor's, Mario was overwhelmed with dismay. The only one of his brothers who had never gone north, nothing he had heard had prepared him to walk among these masses of people, looking for one face. He asked at a Cuban grocery and was finally directed to the boarding house, a narrow brick building from which a woman's voice, loud and throaty and aggressively cheerful, could be heard from the sidewalk admonishing a boarder to wash up quick and come have a cafecito. He knocked, and the woman flung the door open and greeted him with the same volcanic friendliness.

"¡Buenas noches! Aaahh, el maridito de Delia. Entra." He stepped into the small foyer hung with coats.

"Flooora. ¿A donde dijo Delia que iba?" A thin, elderly woman stepped out of a doorway down the hall and examined Mario for several minutes before answering.

"Avanza, que se te pasma!" the woman who had let him in laughed in her booming voice. "Tell him quick, before he shrivels up!"

"Club Diamante, con Rosi." Doña Flora finally replied, and turned her back with a sniff, going back to whatever room she had emerged from.

"Dai Mon Clab, Dai Mon Clab," Mario muttered under his breath, pulling his brother Ignacio's coat closer against the growing chill. It was September, and Nacho, who was home for the moment, had assured him it wouldn't be that cold yet. It was dark and windy and the streets were full of hurrying people in strange clothing. From a cellar door the sound of music, wild, sweet strains of horns and the jazzy tinkling of pianos blew out into the night and he caught a glimpse of a dark skinned woman leaning dizzyingly back over a man's arm then twirling away again out of his sight.

Finally the Diamond Club. A black door with a white diamond painted on it and the same illicit sweetness stealing into the street, and laughter, and the clinking of glasses. Mario opened the door and went in. He paid his ten cents, giving a quick, alarmed glance at the man who took his money. He had been thinking of the Club Social at home, imagining pasodobles performed by carefully dressed young men and ladies, who might work in this huge dirty city, but who celebrated the weekend without loss of dignity. If some of them were darker than was really respectable, he expected these would be the most dignified of all, on their best behavior in the unaccustomed proximity migration gave them to their betters. For all his bashfulness, Mario knew himself to be a Vega.

But this was not Saturday afternoon at the Club Social de Naranjito. It was Friday night in a Harlem speakeasy and the joint was jumping. Women in slinky brilliantly colored dresses, cut low to show a curve of breast, twirled and spun, showed their legs, and even the occasional flash of thigh, as they lay back, tantalizingly, over a man's arm or bent knee, or let themselves be lifted and almost flung through the air. And most of them were dark. Very dark. Then he saw Delia. She was wearing a close-fitted dress of red and silver, covered with shiny red beads, dancing with a tall man who seemed to be the darkest of all, her slim brown ankles whirling, her silver heels kicking up behind her, laughing that same familiar laugh as she rested for a second on the man's arm then flew away from him again.

The tune ended, and she turned, still laughing, and saw him. She walked over easily and stood in front of him, eyes shining.

"Bueno, Mario, quieres bailar?"

Wordlessly he stepped forward as the band struck up a slow dance, something he at least knew how to do. Other couples moved out onto the floor, some of them clutched so tight, Mario had to turn his eyes away. He entered the music as if he were wading into a river whose current might sweep him out to sea. Delia's face was turned to him, alight with fun. Her hand rested on his shoulder, and his on her waist, as he struck out from the shore.

Whatever the garment factory was, is wasn't ladylike. The women had to keep their eyes sharply on the needles, jabbing mechanically through thick folds of fabric, following the long lines and short curves of the seams, unless they wanted to mangle their hands. The racket was deafening and the hours long, but at least there was money at the end of the week, something of her own, however small. She had made friends quickly, with Rosi, Maude, the Irish girl, and Rebecca, whose dark eyes reminded her of Flavia's but who was from Hungary, and a Jew. They were friendships made mostly of smiles and quick help, to pick up a fallen garment, to warn each other of the supervisor's approach, to share a piece of bread and a bite cheese.

Rosi she had met at Doña Flor's boarding house, and Rosi had helped her get the job.

Saturday nights they always went dancing, even though their arms ached from guiding dresses and pants through the rattling machines. Sometimes they went to jook joints full of smoke and forbidden swigs of gin, sometimes to the bright lights of the Savoy, to dance the Lindy Hop with dark young men wearing pressed suits and elegant thin mustaches. Delia rarely thought of the bird filled afternoons she had left behind. It was as if she had stepped out of the shadowy veranda into the blazing sun of day, and could no longer see the cool, still interior beyond the threshold. The slow binding of thread to thread was lost in the rattle and whirl of bobbins, the flying needles that raced through the rippling fabric like silver plows.

Mario had followed her into the glare, but he looked lost, a boy standing abashed at the edges of a brilliant crowd, hat in hand. He had found a room at a nearby boarding house, since Delia shared with another girl and there was no other room available. She left her belongings at Doña Flor's and ate her meals there, but slept with him at his lodgings. Sunday they went to Central Park and walked among trees whose leaves were turning yellow, gold and rich brown. She told him little things about her work, her friends, the clubs and new dance steps she had learned, and he listened, his face serious and still.

What he understood was that she was not coming back. He could not imagine how he'd ever thought that house could contain her. He tried to see himself here, working at something, coming home to a small apartment, having to walk miles to find trees that did not grow in rows, living with the growing cold and incomprehensible speech, surrounded by multitudes of strangers who could not place him, who didn't know or care where he came from, who would not know that his resemblance to his grandfather proclaimed him a Vega and yet he had the eyes of his maternal great-aunt Amalia. He thought he would die of cold, not because of winter, but from the vastness and strangeness of this world into which his Delia had flown.

She seemed to love the crowds of people whose names she didn't know, saw each new encounter as an adventure, laughed at herself as she struggled to communicate with shopkeepers and neighbors. He could not stay, and she could not return, and he didn't know how he would bear it. At night, as she lay, warm and beautiful in his arms, he felt hot tears sting his cheeks and run into her hair.

Each day he walked with her to work. Each evening he was there to escort her home. During the day he wandered, looking at people, smelling and sometimes sampling the strange foods sold from carts or tiny shops. He walked along crowded streets full of stalls offering fruit and fish, hats and coats, and thought he'd never heard so much noise in his life. On Saturday she took him on a trolley to the very end of the city, surrounded by water. They stood there in the bright, chilly afternoon, watching a giant freighter move slowly into the port, a tiny red tugboat pulling and steering. They bought hot pretzels from a man with a cart, and sat on a bench. High above them Mario heard a wild cry, and looking up, saw an arrowhead of large birds, brown wings beating the air.

"Geese", Delia said. "They go south, all the way to Argentina to escape the winter. They would die if they stayed," and she turned to look at him, her gaze direct and sad. She looked back at the geese, steadfastly making their way south, undistracted by the bustling city beneath them as they followed their own path across the sky, ancient and compelling.

"But they return in the spring," he said. "They keep coming back."

In her small room at Doña Flor's there was hardly room to turn around, so she took him into the parlor, and Doña Adelita helped him roll up the carpet. Doña Adelita put a disk on the Victrola, and to the wailing and trumpeting of horns, the thrumming of the base, and voices that tantalized, wept, rejoiced, summoned, Delia taught him how to dance. He moved stiffly at first, but as the afternoon grew dark, and evening lights came on, he began to swing and sway as she instructed, and soon they were whirling around the room, endangering the glass fronted cupboards where Doña Flor kept her best china.

She saw him off at the pier. As the steamship whistle blew deafeningly above his head, he held onto the railing, eyes fixed on her. She stood very still, wearing the simple white dress he had bought her, with eyelet lace at the collar, and a dark brown coat. Once she waved. When he could no longer see her, he went below.

"I couldn't find her" he told his mother, the two brothers who were at home, and all the wives. He didn't seem sad any more.

"Good," said Doña Inés. "We won't speak of her again."

Mario worked dutifully at the family business, and he seemed content. He never took up with anyone in town. But twice a year he packed a small suitcase and went away for a month's vacation. If his family assumed he had a woman somewhere, he said nothing to contradict it. Once Merce, cleaning his room, found a red silk rose among his ties. Doña Inés had long been laid to rest, and they had lost Flavia to consumption, but there was still a house full of de la Vegas when Mario died in 1962. Merce was the only one who was not surprised when the florist delivered six dozen red roses, with a card that said "Thanks for the dance, my love. Delia."

The Memory Papers

An Iranian woman in the underground against the Shah was caught and jailed. She kept herself from telling them, her torturers, the names they wanted from her, by saying to herself repeatedly, "I don't know anyone. I don't remember anyone. I don't know any names." It worked. She doesn't. Still.

I don't remember names. Forget faces, book titles, forget, too, if a person I once knew, who greets me in the street, was friend or enemy. What do you make of this? Is this a dangerous trait of mine, or, al contrario, the first step in forgiving?

I wander in a fog trying to remember if I should remember who that person is, if she was someone who confided in me. People say things that sound familiar. Has anybody told me that before? I disconcert myself by mistaking one of my neighbors for the other. When I discover it, one half minute into my mistake, I sense something, maybe time and space, shift or crack and then recover. Then nausea.

This is my complaint: Everybody else's memory is like the overloaded closet in Fibber Magee and Molly: you open up the closet door and everything comes tumbling out into the hall.

My memory is like the family cat when company comes, hides beneath the bed or slips out the door and is gone. Stays en parranda for three nights in a row, returning thin, dirty, grey. Shy, scrawny, and scarce, my memory.

Take this in evidence: I always know where every cup, plate, spoon, and saucepan goes, how to cook sofrito, how to crochet, what I saw fifty years ago as I was wheeled into the operating room: bright lights, white tiles, white masks and metal apparatus. I had forgotten that I'd invented the drosophila trap that scientists use now, but when I was reminded, knew at once why I had used a juice can, ripe bananas, cardboard and a glass vial. I remember with certainty a million *things*, never forget them, or the constant changes I make in their circumstances. Things are more benign than people, perhaps, less frightening. I usually, often, sometimes remember things.

The case against my mother goes like this. She had the franchise. Memory was her domain. It was not just me. My sister, too, was told she didn't remember right, a constant stream of "Let me tell you what really happened. It was your father who started it. No te recuerdas?" and "No, Sari, how could you be so wrong? You and your sister were never left alone." A flood of "No era así, esto es lo que pasó...No te recuerdas?" "Don't you remember your cousin?" whom I'd never met, or who'd come from Puerto Rico once when I was three. My mother's was a world of endless relatives, relationships with everyone in Puerto Rico, with the whole damn planet, by a link, I'm sure, through a marriage in Toa Alta or Manati four generations back, and to her dying day she really didn't understand that I could not possibly know and didn't care.

What I knew with certainty was that everyone I met when I was young had come to New York City's streets from somewhere else. My world required only a simple passport to link the children in this place to me: where are your parents or your grandparents from? A single document. No need for endless meandering through stores of dead relations, lists of begats, memories of marriages: *Gilberto el*

*que se caso con Cuqui la de Maria. Maria Cruz naturally not Maria
Gonzales whose mother was a Betancourt and the Betancourts don't you
remember are related to the Diaz' in a strange and old and fascinating
way ... No te recuerdas?*

No. She remembers for all of us. But you must not forget, I spoke
another language, not this one, with its Anglo-Saxon sounds hissing
and popping in a soft sea of Latin syllables. "S'vey, s'vey." I mim-
icked it, the surging ocean of gringo noises that surrounded me as I
was carried high above that New York City world in Mami's arms.
I learnt that place in Spanish, the Puerto Rican kind whose words
have rounded corners, their s's and their t's removed like thorns from
the rosy softness of their wide open vowels. I don't remember anything that happened to me before I went to school, to kindergarten,
to be shifted into English gear. All those youngest years, whatever
memories I might have kept of play and falls and food and laps, are
locked away in that baby language and nothing in my adult speech
has turned the key.

I don't know if this explains it all. I only know that I was older
and it was Central Park and I was with my uncle in a playground,
but what—that's what I don't know—was I doing walking along
that row of wildly careening swings each with a heavy child straining higher and higher, feet swung sharply forward as they dashed
toward me, legs tucked under as they darted back. I only know I
was so close that as one strong girl pumped past me, her raised legs
skimmed my hair. But that was not the end of it because the corner
of the hard wooden seat she sat on cracked into my skull, quivering
my brain, cutting my scalp and letting loose the blood that lurks
there, longing to run free. My uncle, who was there to keep me safe,
who should have yelled or pulled me out—well, what are grownups
for?—walked me, bleeding wetly into his handkerchief, the two long
blocks to home.

We know, now, that when you're young, and the unspeakable is done to you, you do not speak. You split the unsafe unbearableness cleanly, with the cleaver of your will, into separate individual portions of personality, or, instead, you cut your mind off at the source, leaving memory to drip unnoticed from the wound. So when I face the blank of those early years, I brood on all the men who moved so easily through all those rooms I can't describe, in buildings I've been only told about. East 106th Street. A furnished room where I once sucked my hungry mother's milk. Lexington Avenue on the hill above the Greek Orthodox church. Ninety-ninth street somewhere. A-Hundred-And-Second Street and Madison. And all those other places no one now remembers, not just me.

My parents were a way-station on the line from Naranjito to America or from *ay dios mio what cold, que frio*, back to home. I don't remember all of them, just one here and one there, but they were legion, cousins, uncles, my parents' childhood friends. I don't remember. Please, someone, tell me, do I wrong them, do I worry needlessly, or did one, any of them, stuff his swollen penis in my tiny mouth, rub his rough finger in my soft slit, lay his huge and heavy body down on top of me? And if he did, then tell me—where? And when? And who?

What do you think of this? My father told me it was my mother's sisters who put ideas into her head—false memory they'd call it now—ignoring what I knew from childhood, what I'd witnessed, what I won't forget. He said it earnestly, in spite of pictures I still own, pictures my mother showed the court that granted her a divorce, of her swollen limbs, blue and black and yellow from the blows. My father chose not to remember.

"Your father stomped upon your naked adolescent toes," my mother said to me a year or so before she died. "You sat," she said, "on the cover of the toilet seat." I have no way of knowing, I've never had, if what she said was true. I don't remember.

But I knew all that I ever needed to: I hated childhood. I have distilled those years into these words and said to anyone who listened that I wanted only to grow up and old. I celebrated like another birth the day I counted as many years away from Papi's hurtful hands (and feet?) and Mami's wicked tongue as I had waited, wanting to get free.

My friends are getting older. They all complain they don't remember well. They stand there, they say, on the bottom step, with no idea of what they came down for. I'm getting old, they quip and laugh. The experts say it isn't so. Memory's not a rat. It doesn't leave you like a sinking ship at forty-five. You stood there at the bottom of those very stairs ten or twenty years ago. But now you have the myth of age, the stories of decay, decrepitude and disease to fall back on. The laughter's nervous. The joke, you think, is on you.

I've always been ashamed of not remembering, of not knowing. It's only now, when practically all my friends have caught up, think age has done this to them, are exclaiming "I'll forget my own name next!"—it's only now, in their company, that I can reach behind the shame and cry.

Unseen

1

*In which Marucha is
introduced, but doesn't
exactly appear.*

Marucha del Carmen Cruz had been invisible for many years. Nevertheless, she had married, borne three children, kept house, edited a socialist journal, studied arts and letters, home decorating, computer programming, community ecology, law and French. She'd cooked, cleaned, sewed, helped the children with their algebra homework, kept a sixteen-volume journal, lost twenty pounds and gained five. Her house was full of the products of her hands, mind, and body, and the objects of her care: small terra cotta busts, crisp doilies in natural linen, a tropical landscape in silks and wools, a six year old girl playing with Legos, two political novels, thirty-seven poems and a play, a dreamy ten year old boy with long legs, a half-dozen lace-edged pillowcases, thirteen dresses, one independent adolescent with small breasts, and endless sketches, recipes, scribbles, notes, letters, dogs, plants, and cats.

She was invited everywhere. Her quiet un-presence presented a cool contrast to the more usual company: loud, contentious, hard drinking and foul smoking, filling the air with harsh laughter and sweaty hands and feet.

She was an excellent hostess, thoughtful, self-effacing and nurturing. Pale young lawyer, mustachioed cultural gurus, callow revolutionaries, mathematical near geniuses, and multicolored social butterflies of all sexes lunged against her upholstered furniture and hand woven pillows, amongst her statuettes and doilies, drinking, sneering, laughing, shouting, eating, necking, destroying reputations, puncturing egos and generally enjoying themselves. She moved softly among them, extinguishing cigarettes, replenishing drinks, re-refilling plates, extracting stilettos, applying band-aids, and restoring shoes, unseen and unheard.

Yes, and unappreciated. Sometimes, recently, she had noticed this. It made her feel very sad. But sadder still was her solitude as a thinker and artist. Why just this month she had completed her verse docudrama on Nigerian women's birthing practices, and she yearned to show it to someone, to share it, to receive praise and criticism. Her drawers were full of experiments, like her algebraic proof in watercolor. She had shown it to her husband. He had sort of liked it and sort of appreciated it, but he was a more superhighway sort of thinker, and her meanderings in the graveled back roads of the mind sort of puzzled him. She needed a wider audience.

But she was invisible. The friends who filled their house didn't notice her. She often tried to join in their discussions on the political future of their island home of San Felipe; did so with verve and energy. Really! The hopes these experienced young revolutionaries placed on the next election, their fresh-minted faith in that old sin-vergüenza they were putting up for office. And in this country where every man with a political corpuscle in his bloodstream mentally refurnished La Casa Blanca while he shaved in the morning, and rehearsed the betrayal of his supporters in his best English while he brushed his teeth. She told them so, reminded them that while Don Alonzo was ancient history, Pedro del Campo de Fuego was just last year.

She could have saved her breath. Papo and Willie and Manolo started a shouting argument in High Left Jargon right in the middle of her second sentence and drowned out even her thoughts. She sat there, carefully shredding a paper napkin, while the argument waxed and waned and waxed again, and Manolo stormed out of the living room and slammed the garden gate, and screeched down the street, farting out angry exhaust fumes.

She was angry, too, but more than that, she was thoughtful. They were going to do it again, back another presidential hopeful anxious for his turn at political corruption. These were the intelligent men that led their political movement, and they were fools.

She wasn't. And they didn't hear her. They drank her coffee and her Cuba Libres, ate her cheese and crackers, smoked her cigarettes and dirtied her sofa, her table, her bathroom, but they didn't see her. At all.

Occasionally they'd nod toward the corner they thought she was in, (often when she was standing right in front of them.) Or they'd ask Miguel how Marucha and the kids were doing, (even though she was sitting at Miguel's side.) Or they'd send Christmas felicitations with special greetings to Marucha y la cría, but that was all. Several times she was hurt rather badly when one or the other of them tried to walk right through her and knocked her down. She'd gotten very good at jumping out of the way quickly when any of them got up to use the bathroom or started to sit down on her. It kept her physically fit, but in a permanent state of mild anxiety.

She was anxious about more that the knocks and bruises she was agilely avoiding. She was beginning to get worried about herself, her descending self-esteem and how it affected her work. Usually when she finished a project she had sixteen waiting in the wings and her biggest problem was which to choose. Now she had none. She seemed to be losing her zest for creating. At first she had thought it was middle age. But no, that was silly. Look at Don Rudolfo at fifty-six or John Phillip at forty-three. They were churning out their paintings and essays faster and better than ever. What they had that she didn't was visibility. They couldn't walk down the street without parents nudging their children and telling them, "Mira, querido, there's a great man. Look well at him. Follow his example. He's a credit to his country. A great man..." And the attention each new painting or essay received! Marucha would sell her family for one sixteenth of that attention, for one one-hundredth, for any at all.

But attention required visibility. Yes, visibility. Marucha, after all the long years of invisibility, wanted to be noticed. And not having any other project in the works at the moment, Marucha turned her attention to this one desired end: to become visible. To be seen.

2

In which the supporting
actors take a reluctant bow.

Miguel sat, large and long and bearded, looking pontifical. He sat silently in a large wicker rocker that his wife Marucha had made for him from directions given in the January issue of *Casas y Cosas*. He was a man who spoke very little, very softly, very seldom. But he was a Very Important Man, Highly Visible, Very Heard. Everything stopped when he spoke. The omnipresent coughers and spitters held their coughs and swallowed their spit. Jokes stopped in mid-punch line, hairy hands on mid-thigh. Only the soft sound of reverent breathing and the slight scratchings of a worn out ballpoint recording his words could be heard beneath his voice.

"Ahh." Miguel breathed quietly, sighing to ease his hurt and his fear. He didn't look hurt of frightened. He looked Wise. And his friends and comrades felt comforted by this Wise Look and Wise Sigh. They held their breaths for several minutes while they waited for any words that might follow that slight sound. Moncho and Luisito became quite blue, a pretty blue, speckled with pink. But none came, so they sucked in large gulps of air and resumed the battle that passed for conversation amongst them.

Miguel held himself very stiffly, very still. His posture gave him a majestic look, as if he were above the itchings and squirmings of human flesh, as if he were all the Great Mind and hardly sordid body at all. He look on Benignly, Wisely, as Manolo questioned Willie's intelligence and Willie questioned Toti's wit.

Miguel held himself rigid because he was afraid he would break. After years of having his most superficial word treated as the most profound wisdom and his inner thoughts and feelings ignored as if they were totally non-existent, he had come to believe that he had no inner thoughts and feelings, that he was a shell, hollow and empty inside. He felt like the cheap celluloid dolls they gave as prizes at coconut shies in the pre-plastic 1940's: thin, brittle, easily dented, even more easily cracked. As he became more and more important he felt emptier inside, thinner and more vulnerable outside. He spoke less and less often about lesser and lesser matters and held himself more and more carefully and was in consequence seen as More Important than ever before.

Miguel was important to Marucha but not Very Important at all. He was kind, he was clever, and she had loved him for many years. Better yet, he had loved her for many years. Of course, he saw her, spoke to her, touched her, made love to her. He knew where she was in the room, in the house, at all times. Since he spoke so little and moved even less, he could hear the smallest, most distant sounds, so that he derived comfort from her heartbeat while she slept in another room, from the soapy slither of her sponge when she bathed, even when he was miles away in his office. The student apprentices on his editorial staff would notice a small twitch of a smile and wonder how they had pleased him. What had pleasured him was the scratch of Marucha's nails at the itch on her calf, or the flip of buttons as they slipped into the holes in her blouse.

As Marucha tucked her blouse into her slacks she felt his pleasure. Unlike their friends and comrades, Marucha saw and felt Miguel's inner world. She lived in a sea of his feelings, felt them wash in and out, turn stormy, turn calm, become choppy, become slick and grey and threatening. It was a kind of weather and she took it for granted, noticed vaguely that the temperature had dropped today and she would need to cover up to keep warm or that the storm was ending and the sun was coming out and it would be good weather for putting her feelings out to air.

Today Marucha was humming softly as she vacuumed the guest room, made the bed up with the ecru lace spread that had taken her a year to crochet. It was one of Rolando's favorites. He was coming to stay with them while he looked for a place to live. He'd been living in New York City for they last year ever since he decided that Bogotá was no better that Ciudad Mexico or San Francisco for his intellectual and emotional health. Now he was coming back to try his native San Felipe once more, to give it a chance to heal and restore him.

"I wonder what he's into now?" she thought as she smoothed the pillow. "He's so unexpected. Let's see...the last time it was Yiddish love poetry. No, that was earlier. Soapstone sculpture? French novels? Arabic historiography?" It was hard to keep track but never mind. Whatever it was, it would be exciting, fun. Life with Rolando in the house was like living in a bottle of champagne: tickly, bubbly, intoxicating.

It was strange, wasn't it, that Rolando, like Miguel, saw her – a good deal of the time, anyway. And like herself, he noticed Miguel's feelings – at any rate, rather often. Not all the time, because Rolando had little attention to spare from the great problem that preoccupied him night and day, that stopped him in the middle of carrying the soup spoon to his mouth, as he lowered himself onto the toilet, or as he explained the inner workings of a Central Asian ballad form. He would frown all over his body, still his breathing, even his heart, and look in, far in, all the way into himself, leaving nothing but his motionless form to remind Marucha that Rolando had been there with them.

Rolando was trying to discover what was wrong with him. Something was wrong, that was sure. Everyone agreed on that. But what was wrong with Rolando? All his friends and relations, all their acquaintances and comrades, asked that question regularly, sometimes acidly, sometimes amusedly, sometimes solemnly. They called meetings to ask and answer and debate it. Manolo was even writing an essay on it tentatively titled "The Rolando Question, a Dialectical Approach."

What <u>was</u> wrong with him? Marucha wasn't too sure. She rather liked Rolando as he was. She would have liked him a lot more without The Question but other that that he seemed a much nicer person to her than all the questioners. Sometimes she wondered if that wasn't a mere selfishness and self-interest. After all, he saw and heard and appreciated her. He danced the merengue with Amanda, the adolescent, played beisbol with Felicia, the six year old, and listened appreciatively to Gilbertito's moaning on the oboe. And he made Miguel laugh, small quivering laughs that made the rocking chair rock gently.

She had to agree with Luisito and Manolo. Rolando did change interests and studies and professions rather often. He moved such a lot, too. And he had so many infatuations and love affairs and marriages and disillusionments and break-ups. It was all a bit dizzying to watch. But she didn't like their calling him Rodando for his rolling stone existence. She didn't like the imitations they did of him whenever they got together. She didn't like their using him as the universal bad example with tuttings and head shakings and puckered lips. She didn't like their hilarity when he wrote of a new lover, a new city, a new interest. It made her feel slightly ill, as though she'd eaten something on the edge of spoiling.

Marucha took a last look around the room. It looked welcoming, the smooth bed, the large reading lamp, a bedside table for Rolando's bottles and pens and pads and books and bits of stone or plants or weavings or whatever he was carrying and fingering and examining and analyzing at the moment. A good desk – that was Gilbertito's who didn't use it for anything better than parking his shoes, schoolbooks, dirty underwear and dirtier dishes. Gilbertito kept his bed smooth and clean and did his homework on it, received guests on it, slept, ate, lived on it. He could spare the desk. Rolando would set up a typewriter on it or canvases or a bookbinding press. Maybe it would be a loom this time. She smiled and closed the door.

In which the plot
bubbles, boils, thickens
and is stirred.

Dinner was a delight. Rolando had brought cream cheese, lox, chopped liver and four dozen bagels in his hand luggage and they spread them out on the table and cut and smeared and ate and laughed. Rolando insisted that they drink hot black tea in tall glasses and sip it through sugar cubes in true Eastern European style while he told them Jewish jokes. Gilbertito burnt his tongue, Amanda kept dropping her sugar cube in her tea, Felicia refused to eat anything but cream cheese on sugar, Miguel smiled gingerly around large mouthfuls and Marucha held her stomach because it hurt from so much laughing.

She experienced a small quiver of regret as she looked around at their happy faces. She'd invited a good number of their friends for after dinner drinks to welcome Rolando home. She wished she hadn't, wished they could just be the six of them and the cats, dogs and turtle tonight sitting out on the veranda in the tepid tropical night. But Rolando had asked to see Manolo and Luisito and Marta and the others, the old gang, in fact, and Marucha was ready to begin Operation Visibility so she'd made a few phone calls, sent a few cards, a pigeon and a wire.

She had decided that she needed to have objective information on the process of invisibilization. This get-together would provide her with data. She'd considered using a tape recorder and rejected that. She always forgot to turn the tape over and in any case she didn't want a complete replay of the evening. She would take notes. When she was young she'd spent several months in a monkey colony recording their behavior on large sheets of lined paper with special hieroglyphics and could record behavioral interactions and displays of emotion with great economy and efficiency. She pulled out a few yellowing sheets, sharpened her pencil, put out a self-service bar on the porch and resolved to let her guests cope with their thirst as best they could without her usual tender care.

"Mira, Marucha..." Rolando was juggling three bagels and balancing another on his nose while the two dogs barked. The bell rang, the bagels fell, the dogs rushed off to the front door. They were here.

Manolo arrived first, smiling gently, his kind eyes shedding soft love at Miguel, at the dogs, the children, the other side of the room where he imagined Marucha to be. He smiled at Rolando, and asked him, quietly, lovingly, whether he was still the utter failure, the intolerable bore, he had been when he left. Rolando smiled back, said yes, that he found Manolo unchanged, too, gratified for what still seemed a loving welcome. The acid of Manolo's words always took time to eat away at their sugared crust. Hours later, Rolando would jump back and clutch his heart with the pain of them. Manolo's friends were known for their eccentric acrobatics, their unexpected, sour, hurt looks.

Luisito was coming up the walk, arm in arm with Marta. His small feet in their elegant shoes, his neat hands making cutting gestures, his thin mouth smiling with just the right level of superiority, his bright eyes looking deeply into Marta's eyes for her weakness, her mistakes, her indulgences, her despised humanity. His cleverness gleamed from his well-shined shoes to his carefully curled hair. It twinkled from his bright white teeth. It slipped off his tongue at Marta, at Miguel standing largely by the front door. It spattered into the room ahead of him like electricity. Even the dogs felt it, their hair lifting off their ears and backs, so that they looked like thin-needled porcupines.

Marta swept in, oblivious of the charge in the air around her, her eyebrows raised, the right side of her large, lovely mouth tipped up, her be-ringed hand gleaming against her shawl. She always looked straight at Marucha when she walked into the house. And now she stared somewhat blankly at her, as she greeted everyone with a vague gesture of her free hand. It had always puzzled Marucha that Marta seemed to see her and yet didn't. The fact was that Marta was cutting Marucha dead, looking deliberately away from the corner she imagined her to be in, and by the perverse logic of calculated disdain, managed to point her nose unerringly to the exact place where Marucha stood or sat or moved. Marta would have shuddered had she known. She would have felt herself contaminated by Marucha's ugliness, by her empty life, her superficial pursuits, her political nonexistence. She despised Marucha's life—hanging onto the coattails of the Great Man, mingling with his brilliant friends, basking in the light of Marta's own well-groomed beauty, her revolutionary acumen, her cosmopolitan sophistication. Not looking at Marucha was one of the high points of her all too social life.

Paquito had slithered in unobserved, had taken hold of Miguel's right arm, and clamped his mouth to Miguel's right ear. He was asking him the most important questions of all, the answers to which he needed for his growth, the advance, the meteoric rise he planned all his waking moments and in most of his dreams.

"How do you choose great thoughts?"

"Do you arrange your dreams to give you brilliant insights?"

"Is sex good or bad for the development of the brain?"

"When do you do your best thinking?"

"Does constipation affect your productivity?"

"How do you decide what to say?"

"Can you..."

Miguel slowly worked himself loose from Paquito's grasp and followed everyone onto the veranda, while Paquito still grasped convulsively, still whispered urgently into the softly charged air.

As the others straggled past Paquito, they congregated in small groups wherever they found themselves, exchanging stale news and repeating old libels. Slowly their thirst drove them toward the veranda. There they asked Miguel how Marucha was. When they saw the bar with its empty glasses and full bottles, they asked *where* Marucha was. When they'd sat and talked and got up and talked and were parched and disgruntled, they asked where in carajo Marucha was. And when they slapped in the rum, splashed in the soda, and threw in the ice, they wondered que'n diablo, coño, carajo was she up to?

She was down on a footstool in the corner behind the couch, sitting on her hands. She could feel the embroidery engraving deep marks on the skin of her fingers, and the remarks putting deep color in her face. When her guests were settled, more or less, she moved to the porch rail and sat herself where she could see everyone, in full view of their unseeing eyes.

The party was well launched. Marucha could tell by the sound, a noise made up of greetings and chewings and inquiries, of ice on glass and backslaps and triumphant cries, of the squeaks of furniture and kisses deposited half an inch off the offered cheeks. A sound, too, of laments. Laments about the state of the movement, the state of the country, the state of the university, the failure of the latest alliances, the breakdown of the copier, the bankruptcy of the radical publisher. Laments sotto voce, laments in B flat with accompaniment, laments singly and laments in chorus.

Then a general movement—to the drinks, to the bathroom, to another group, another chair—and more laments: laments about friends, about their ideas, their politics, their finances, their marriages, their children, their love affairs, their clothes, their personal habits. Which brought the conversations neatly round to Rolando, and six or seven of them sat or stood around and talked at him.

"Well, now…" (Small smile.) "Have you finished your thesis yet? Let's see…it was about some obscure literature, "

And before Rolando could do more than start his "Well, see, it's this way…",

"Mira, muchacho, how long are you staying in Puerto Nuevo? Do you think that this time you could stay long enough to…"

"Rolando! It's come to my ears that you've been toying with Maoist notions which…"

"…if she's as ugly as the last one. Remember, Marta? All ears and hair…"

"…to buckle down and accomplish something. You're not getting any…"

"Paris! Positively last century. And being a hippie in San Francisco, I imagine!"

"…should give some serious though to…"

"…wives in all. Six alimonies, no less, so obviously…"

"..no moss and less sense. You know nothing about Puerto Nuevan conditions now."

"Incredibly, irresponsibly childish..."

Rolando had at first tried to answer one or another or all of them, but there was never any break or breathing space where his words could be inserted. So he told himself. He explained to himself about his thesis, his travels, his political line, his love life. He looked for Marucha or Miguel, to tell them, but he was surrounded by bodies standing two deep about his chair. He tried to stand, and pushed on the chair arm, levered himself halfway up, and then...

Went still.

One arm reaching out to make a space between Toño and Marta, the other on the arm of the chair, he delved in and in and into himself, to a yet deeper place, to discover where and how and what was wrong with him. Seeking, searching, digging into his feelings, he was dismayed to discover his boyhood selfishness in eating all the mango jelly his mother had put in the cupboard for his father's morning toast, his destructiveness in breaking his older sister's newest doll with his rattle, his thoughtlessness in crying for a diaper change in the middle of the night, his greediness for demanding the breast only hours after his exhausted mother had given birth to him, his cruelty for tearing his mother's perineum with his much too large head while emerging, his aggressiveness in hiccupping and kicking and turning, and disturbing his mother's sleep all through those endless months, his laughably ironic sense of timing in getting conceived when he did, his...

And as he pursued his own worthlessness all the way back into the ovum, the sperm, that went into making up that first cell of Rolandoness, he became dizzy, staggered, looked around a little stupidly and sat down.

They were telling Rolando jokes.

"Did you hear the one about Rolando at the airport, picking his next home by throwing dice?"

"How many Rolandos does it take to screw in a light bulb? None. You screw in Rolando instead."

"How does Rolando get into his pants in the morning?"

"How does Rolando make love in a strange city?"

"How does Rolando know who he's sleeping with at night?"

Rolando at the university, registering. Rolando giving a party. Rolando drunk, or sober, or eating, or...

Marucha had stopped making strange marks in her social inventory. She was doodling instead, a little unhappy face with giant tears suspended below it, like deformed bodies. She filled in each tear carefully, while she thought, "They don't see him either. No, they do see him, they see his body, shake his hand, even. Not like me. But somehow they don't see him at all, only an idea of him, a shape at which to throw their wicked darts. And he disappears...inside himself...sort of. He rolls up and rolls away...kind of." She drew the eyes meticulously: iris, lids, eyelashes. "As if they had waved a magic wand at him."

Marucha started on the hair, long and straight in places, and in ringlets and curlicues in others. "And I used to think them charming and interesting. Not ever kind, really, except...they did listen to Miguel so flatteringly and they seemed sophisticated and knowledgeable.

They did seem knowledgeable, and earnest, and serious. And they were, or had been, politically active, most of them, and so militant. They still are...some of them...somewhat. Have they changed so much? Has Puerto Nuevo changed? Have I?"

A discontent and restlessness nudged through the small crowd on the open veranda. There were shiftings and shufflings, rubbings and rustlings. It was just past the halfway point of the evening, the time between the excitement and satisfaction of exchanging routine for other people's food, faces and rooms, and the return to the emptiness of the car, the sameness of the habitual partner, or the dull familiarity of the new one. This was that time, and they were bored: bored with themselves and each other, bored with their host, with the company of a Very Important Person who didn't smile and approve and slap their backs, who didn't utter, not even a theoretical breakthrough or a fragment of a future masterpiece. Bored with their hostess who wasn't there, who wasn't all there, who wasn't what she should be, who wasn't all they'd expected, who never quipped, told racy stories, or looked deep into their eyes with appreciation. Bored with Rolando's unchanging changeability. Bored with the same old jokes they'd told for ten years. Bored with the plants, the furniture, the air, the climate, the time of day.

Marucha's drawing was becoming darker. The pencil lines were overwhelming the yellow spaces. She thought, "and Miguel either. They don't see him. Well, they see his form, his size, his importance...But no, it's not *his* importance, not even *his* form. It's someone they've made up. Someone who doesn't look like my Miguel in the least. Look at them now, how they ignore him when he isn't saying anything they can write down. And they have no idea what he's feeling, or even that he *can* feel.

Just then there was another of those shifts in the gathering, the tectonics of the social scene, and whole groups drifted and clashed and threw out islands and consolidated into new continents. A large shelf of them hovered discontentedly by the now depleted drinks table, talking in low, penetrating whispers about the empty rum bottle, the melted ice, the crumpled napkins, the crumb-filled plates, the butt-filled ashtrays. The veranda now looked and smelled like all their hangouts: the Party headquarters on Calle Lucera, or the newly popular bar in old Puerto Cristo. Stale smoke, spilled rum, fresh sweat, and mingled vestiges of aftershave and perfume permeated the rumpled room. A woman's voice rose above the whispers, complaining about Marucha's housekeeping and hospitality, how they'd been going downhill, she'd see it coming, hadn't she said it... menopause...sucking Miguel dry..., while two men's voices successfully drowned her out with competing hypotheses of incipient alcoholism and chronic depression.

In a far corner, Miguel sat withholding speech from several worshipful young men at his feet. He was angry at what he was hearing. Miguel felt an overwhelming urge to speak, to berate them, to point out their rudeness, unkindness, ungratefulness. But his feelings were too strong and the topic too important to him, so nothing came out. Instead he became overwhelmingly sad. He sat, clamped in his habitual immobility, looking impassive, while he wept internally, at the hurtfulness of his friends, at Rolando's unhappy self-punishment, at Marucha's isolation and disparagement, wept at Luisito's thwarted idealism, wept so steadfastly, so thoroughly, so feelingly, that clouds formed around him. The air became thick and heavy with moisture. It fogged the eyeglasses of the nearsighted, and the fashionable shades of the farsighted. It dripped off the cold tumblers and the ice bucket.

Marucha put down her pencil and wiped her hands on her skirt. "..or each other. Marta doesn't see anyone but herself, and that not very clearly. Toño doesn't have a clue about this country. He only knows what's in books about other places. And Conchita..."

The happy voices were now loud enough to penetrate even Marucha's absorption. They were indulging in an orgy of Marucha trashing. The hair on her legs rose slowly as she listened. The prickles of heat now stung in the folds behind her knees and the insides of her elbows. A small chorus was describing her ineptitude, backed up by an orchestral rendition of her moral turpitude, while isolated voices broke in here and there with sharp notes about her mediocrity.

True, she was the center of attention. True, they were aware of her existence. But her gratitude for this small mercy shriveled in the waves of heat that rose, like hot flashes, up her body, her throat, her face. She began muttering inaudibly, and her body and mind began slowly emptying out her stoppered store of ancient, unrealized anger, not only at Rolando's friends, and Miguel's and her guests, but at all of them: at the hundreds of self-important, brilliant brains, sophisticated snobs, and macho militants who had elbowed her ribs, stomped on her instep, jabbed their gesticulating fingers in her eyes, twisted her arm, poked, pushed and punched her out of their way to the greater glory of MANkind, and never mind her tendings and cleanings and cookings and care, never mind her sorrows and comforts and Sunday sleep, never mind her periods and pregnancies, her babies and toddlers and teenagers, and never mind that she was never consulted and wasn't allowed to speak, wasn't heard or wanted.

She was quite hot now, and fanned herself with her scribbled pad. Her muttering rose to a high whine and became just barely audible. A voice like that of an abandoned spirit, disembodied and thin, floated above the room, and a palpable warmth lapped out from among the bromeliads.

The voice went on objecting, exposing, denouncing. It produced an unpleasant, formless, unmusical tone. Only occasional words and phrases could be distinguished.

"...man-o-war of the revolution, all jelly and sting..."

"...mouseturds..."

"...fleas..."

Now her voice became louder and harsher and the room was filled with a low, rumbling sound, a pervasive vibration that set the dogs to chasing their tails, and the guests to clutching each other's arms and looking behind them suspiciously in the now oppressive heat. "Oh, it's too much! It's too much. How could I have taken all this, from all of them, for all these years? How could I? They're as blind as cave bats. They walk around my house and their homes and the country and don't see a thing. Not me, not each other, not anyone or anything else. They're full of their brilliant shit theories, and their vanguard shit role, and their male shit importance. And these women, heavy with their vital secondary supporting auxiliary roles. The ones that weren't being little pseudo-males, that is. None of them realize that they're as thoughtless as chickens, as cruel as piranhas, acquisitive as crows, as slovenly as chimpanzees.

"Oh, and some of you," and now she looked straight at her uneasy guests, "some of you only want a revolution so you can move into important positions and big houses and big power. Your envy of the tyrants oozes out of your nostrils, green and snotty. You! You pretend that I'm inaudible, that I'm invisible, but it's *your* ignorance, *your obliviousness.*"

She stopped when she heard what she'd said. She stopped in amazement and joy and then anger, real anger like she'd never known before, surged through her. Anger that felt like two hundred and fifty volts, that they had done this to her, acting as if *she* was unseeable, as if *she* had a voice that couldn't be heard. Anger at herself for being such a fool as to allow them to ignore her, such a coward and fool as to retreat into invisibility, to become what they'd decreed. Oh, she was angry! So angry and hot that she developed a glow, a watery light like a bottle of fireflies. Then a firmer light, (fireflies packed shoulder to shoulder in a small, confined, glass space,) so that Marta and Manolo and some others facing the veranda rail could dimly see a pale disembodied arm stretched toward them, a finger pointing in accusation.

"You haven't seen me for ten years, but I've seen you. I've finally seen you, seen how silly you are, silly and dangerous and hypocritical. Oh! You have tongues like stingrays. You strut and posture like red-assed baboons. You leave broken bits of lives in your wake like tidbits of flesh behind frenzied sharks. Let me tell you what you've done, who you've pushed to an early grave, and who is drinking alone tonight because of you."

She began enumerating the sad forgotten people who had inadvertently wandered into their lives, or stepped purposely into their meetings, the ones who left or were left, who were dropped or dropped out. The ones who went away humiliated, the ones who thought they were stupid, past help, the ones who were bitter and no longer believed that any change or improvement was possible, the ones who were drowning in self-pity and alcohol, the ones who were risking death with small vials of pills and getting their stomachs pumped and their psyches investigated, the ones who were apathetic and bored, the ones who were resigned and conventional.

Her sorrow and indignation burned so brightly that she materialized before their astonished eyes, sharp and clear and enraged, enthroned between the spiny leaves and red blooms of her potted plants. Her voice became louder and fiercer, a tornado of a sound, that peppered them with truths that stung like hornets, so that they slapped at their ears and jumped about, waving newspapers at the words that buzzed at them from the air; so that they ran from them, jumped off the veranda, raced through the living room and out the door, past the slow smile that bloomed gently on Miguel's face.

The voice grew and grew, and kept speaking to them even in their cars as they screeched into gear. It grew, and flew after them as they fled as fast as they could, as far as they could. It followed them into their houses, their lives, their beds, their sleep. It crept into their openings, leaving tiny bits of buried truth, like minute parasitic wasp eggs in their skin, in the moist sides of their ears and mouths and assholes, in the walls of their throats, their guts and their stomachs. Truths that wormed their way, ate at them, ate at their substance, for all the rest of their days.

Hurricane

They sang "Pueeertoh Reeeeko" pushing past me in the crowded hallways in their knee socks and plaid skirts, "my hearts devooootion," rushing to beat the passing bell, swinging their book bags against my shins, "let it sink into the OCEAN!", giggling and nudging each other as they slid into their seats for English I, demure, well-behaved girls in soft sweaters and loafers, with tiny gold hearts hanging around their necks on chains. Watching them rush through the hallways in giggling, chattering clusters, I longed for the girls of Matorelli Junior High near Yagrumo, whose companionship I had won so hard, after years of "¡Oye, rubia!" and "¡Americanita!" Where had they gone, with their familiar, gossipy ways, with their loud laughter and sharp argumentative voices, with their "A'e María, mija. No seas tan changa!?" I imagined them through all the sterile afternoons of fluorescent lights and homeroom, dressed in maroon skirts and white blouses, standing together, waiting by side of the road, under the flamboyán, for the público to take them home.

Time unraveled. It whirled past me like the leaves that blew in stormy spirals, whipping round my shins every afternoon on the way home from school. Those long, slow days in Candelarias, where each hour ran into the next and no-one counted them too closely— here they had been diced up and plastic-wrapped. Bells rang every fifty minutes. They rang for exactly four seconds, and then again, four minutes later on the dot. In Candelarias children straggled in to the classrooms as they could. Rain or mud or work on the farm could make us late. Many mornings, missing the bus to Matorelli, I had wandered down the mountain for four hours, arriving in time for lunch. Only a whole day out required a note, and no one made a fuss unless we were gone for days on end, and in coffee season, not even then.

But at this gleaming new school of glass and steel they had more rules than Candelarias had students! Five minutes late meant a pink slip. More than five minutes meant a blue slip, and required a note from home or a talk with an official. Two or more blue slips meant you had to get a green slip and go to detention. No one understood how bewildering all this pointless precision was, how it cut me loose from the sun, and made me forget my body.

If the days were minced into tiny bits, the nights were desolate. It never got dark enough to rest my eyes, never quiet enough to let me stretch my hearing. Cars, buses, people, dogs, garbage cans rattling in the wind, but no rustle of leaves, no hawks' cries, no coquís, no rain pounding on a tin roof. And no distances to look into even when it was day. In each of my sense I was hemmed in. In boots and sweaters and jackets and hats and scarves, I hiked through the growing chill to school each day, through the dizzying strangeness.

It had never occurred to me that my lost home on the crest of the cordillera could evoke anything but envy in girls who had spent all their lives living in this bleak city of wind and brown brick. But they seemed to regard even the air I had once breathed with embarrassment. Homesickness consumed me. I woke from dreams of wild longing, in which the most precious imaginable sweetness slid from my memory. That was the tragedy, not only lost, but forgotten. In my dreams I would pass my truest loves, for whom I had risked everything, and see only strangers. That year the sun vanished from my hair. As winter darkened, so did my coloring. By the new year, I was a brunette, and Anibel Hrosseng Rivera became Annie Rosen, another Jewish faculty daughter being "prepped" for achievement.

Except that I wasn't quite. Couldn't ever be. Much as even the best intentioned of them wished I was.

What did I learn in school? I learned that words that sound like compliments can be daggers: "What an exotic life you've led!" "Your background is so...interesting". I learned that where you stand in the scheme of things can be a coat, not flesh. A coat that can be changed with the season, with the country. In Puerto Rico I was "rubia", and the daughter of privilege. Here I lived at the edge of respectability. I was a foreigner from a "backward" land. In Candelarias my father was both Americano, and rich. Six thousand dollars a year was an associate professor's salary, a third of what the University of Chicago paid, but it was many times more than the profits from a couple of cuerdas of coffee, even in a good year. In Candelarias we looked like the people who owned things, who decided things. We did decide things—who would be hired to clear the hillside, whether or not to notice that Chago had moved the fence again.

In Chicago my mother was a Puerto Rican from Harlem and my father was a Commie Jew who'd been teaching in the Third World. We borrowed money to make ends meet, and my clothing was not in style. In Chicago I was at the low budget end of middle class. My tastes were "unusual". My homesickness was an embarrassment. My name was awkward. The people I moved among were too polite to say the actual word, but when they mangled the syllables of my language, when they deplored my Caribbean expectations of hospitality, when they let me know that my voice was too expressive, my gestures too flamboyant, my friendliness undignified, the word that was in their eyes was SPIK, SPIK, SPIK. It was not a word I knew, but letter by letter, I learned it.

What did I learn in school? That we were handpicked and lucky. Fourteen Black students. Nine Asians, most of them several generations from Asia, a few whose fathers had come from Pakistan or Taiwan to teach, but who knew the difference? Three of what people still called "Spanish" students. A boy from Peru, a girl from Colombia, and me. Twenty six out of twelve hundred.

That being from another country was odd and uncouth, but that *knowing* someone from another country made you sophisticated and cosmopolitan. That being from South America, if your father was an engineer, was tolerable, but being Puerto Rican, from anywhere, no matter what your parents did, was not.

Strange and painful lessons. I learned that we inhabited an island of culture in a sea of savagery. That the university, and our school, its junior partner, nestled in green lawns and black iron fences, was a sanctuary where the human mind was holy, but that just across a strip of grass one block to the south was the jungle ghetto. Outside of our walled satisfactions, they implied, the human mind, if it existed at all, was trapped in useless, violent rage, degraded into relentless self-abuse.

I learned that Black people lived there in brown brick buildings with grey wooden fire escapes, drinking and shooting and mainlining drugs, and killing each other in a gang warfare that had nothing at all to do with us. No said anything about love, or courage, or loyalty. No one asked what it takes to get up every morning in a city that wants you dead and decide to live and keep your child, a lover, a friend alive with you. *No one mentioned the blues.*

The lesson was segregation and assimilation. I learned it in words and in the spaces between words. We were not to go there. It was a bad neighborhood. If we went there we would be hurt because we were, or should be, white. Because we were innocent. There was a dangerous tide of violence and hatred, pounding constantly on the walls of our safety. Be one of us, they said, even if you're second best. The alternative is just too awful.

The lesson was paternalism and irresponsibility. The thing is, they were jealous of us. Because they didn't know how to help themselves. They hadn't had our advantages. Their culture was impoverished. This was for many sad reasons that had come to pass long ago. It was nothing to do with us. We had only ourselves to look out for. We had to train our minds and do well on tests. We had to go for achievement. We would of course vote for liberals when we could vote, and we would be proud of an America in which Martin Luther King could campaign for civil rights. For ourselves though, if we felt strongly about something, we would write letters to our elected representatives. We would be tolerant of the differences which made our country great and not call names. Those of us who were not really white could be credits to our people. We could show America that our people were capable of producing something pretty good if we tried hard.

Because we had so much that was good, we had to be merciful. That fall, a group of us were recruited to be merciful after school. We were taken by bus to a dark, musty building "over there" under the El tracks, to tutor children in reading and math. We were warned not to become friends with them because they would only feel abandoned when we left. We were told to stay impersonal and professional. To dispense learning without love. This was in the best interests of the children. After lessons each child got a boiling cup of weak, mint-flavored instant hot chocolate as a reward. Instead of respect.

The girl I got was a scrawny African-American seven year old who had just moved up from Arkansas and would eagerly clutch my sleeve and whisper stories about the tornadoes she had lived through "back home." Now she lived in a single room with her mother and two babies, with the El ripping past night and day. I tried to get her through the paces of Dick and Jane, all bright and shiny in front of their clean, quiet house, but what I wanted from her was not obedience, but everything she knew about living through disasters. So I let her pluck my sleeve while we both bent our heads under the stern, admonishing eye of the teacher, and I listened while she whispered in my ear.

The nights got colder, the hurrying figures on the street more muffled, the gusting winds carried away the sounds of sirens and gunshots. After a while, things inched back toward a murky spring, slushy streets, lilacs popping open behind their fences, and then it was April, and Memphis, and smoke rising from dozens of hotspots of rage, panic-stricken suburban parents calling the school to have their kids sent home, then, as the sound of smashing glass spread, calling back to say "Stay there!" *Shoot to kill* seemed written across the sooty sky, the blue lights of cop cars flickered along the streets, and "The suspect was running," they said. "The suspect behaved suspiciously, when we threw him up against the squad car, then down on the ground. He resisted"

I wore a black armband to school, and when those warring nations, the two vast gangs, met on the grass across from my school to sign a cease fire for the duration of this lockdown, when a few of the younger boys swaggered into our student lounge in their jackets and berets and put their feet up on the coffee table, while skinny white boys in nice shirts flicked nervous glances their way, and the girls clumped and whispered, looking over their shoulders, I laughed out loud with pleasure. But no one, to look at me, would've thought *boricua cimarrona*. My hair didn't crinkle upwards like my brother's, making him eligible for a wider brotherhood. It hung in dark fronds, framing my crisp English. In a city slashed into territories of black and white, a long train ride from the barrios, off-white girls like me vanished into people's assumptions. It wasn't just the sun that faded from me. Whole continents within me went silent.

One day, sitting in geometry class, it would have been the second year of my confusion, I remember thinking about Shoe Day. It had been the ordeal of each school year for me. On that day, every child in the class was expected to stand up when called on, and tell the teacher her or his family income. Those below a certain level got a free pair of shoes. I always tried to be absent on shoe day, but never succeeded. Each year, I had to stand up and tell my schoolmates that my father earned in a month what some of their families had to live on for half a year. What's more, his paycheck came on the first of the month, irrespective of the weather, while the income that bought my friends their rice and beans and uniforms dribbled in at the mercy of rain and wind and drought. It would take weeks for us all to recover, for the mortification and rage of class to sink back into its bed and leave us room, on its muddy banks, to play.

In the light of my aching loss, I remembered them as they were, awkwardly refusing to enter my parents' house, because it was too much better than their own. Afraid of the flush toilet. Shamefacedly or defiantly begging for my hair bands and pencils, bullying me into giving up my sweets, and mercilessly teasing me for thinking I knew what was in store for me.

I remembered Ramona, who was black, and poor, and beat on by the teachers, who told her she was a stupid girl at least ten times a day, only half the time in words. I never forgot her again. Years later, when I read the nostalgic poetry of other exiles who claimed that racism was not a Puerto Rican failing, because "negra" was an endearment, I wasn't fooled. I remembered Ramona because of what I had seen written in white peoples eyes: school girls with shiny straight hair and courteous, thin lipped mothers, condescending guidance counselors, baton wielding cops, their eyes hidden behind dark shades and visors. I remembered all the times I heard the Candelarias schoolgirls talk about who was pretty and who was dark, who had good hair and who had bad. I knew now that where you stood, and in whose shoes, changed everything about what was visible. You learn what you need to know. In Candelarias, nothing had forced me to recognize the daily, deadly grind of racism. In Chicago, everything did.

There were years of numbness, though. Years when I didn't even dream of home anymore. When I learned how to be what was expected and not volunteer more than what I was asked. Years when politeness coated me like a thin, hard shellac, so that nothing I did was natural. I became a feminist because in those rooms of women leaning intently toward each other, I could *feel* something. Indignation became an anchor. I began to write again. Not the poems and fables of my childhood, but thick, black journals full of emotion, like a howling wind, where I raged and mourned and thought and planned, reaching, with ink stained hands, for the right words, the true things, the clear, bright eye in the center of the storm.

Vivir Para Tí

The afternoon pressed into her like the palm of a huge hand, hot and damp against her thickening body. ¡Ay! Me sofoco. She stood in the doorway, her hand on her hip, watching two hens stalk the dirt, tipping their heads to look for stray kernels of corn. She reached into her pocket for a handful of grain and threw it to them. More chickens came scurrying out from under the bushes. Leaning against the wood she looked out at the hills, falling away softly, stifled, too, by the dense air. The baby pressed relentlessly, hard as a green orange, against her breastbone, crushing her breath.

In the dim room behind her the television droned on to itself, casting a blue light into the corners. The passionate voices and shadowy faces were flattened by the brilliant light. She couldn't remember the characters' names. Was it the two 'o clock novela or the three 'o clock? You didn't remember the people, just the situations. The music rose and then changed abruptly. Luz glanced back over her shoulder into the dark room.

A cheerful young mother and her small daughter, in matching aprons, sat at a table in a brand new kitchen, pouring the best selling brand of tomato sauce into Papá's beans, stirring and singing a little song together. After a moment Papá walked in the door from work, wearing a shirt and tie, smiling and carrying a briefcase. He kissed the wife and child, sat down and tasted the beans, and smiled with satisfaction. Then a dancing tomato sauce can wiggled across the screen and the picture faded. Luz used a different brand.

She walked herself to the stove and lit the flame under a pot of peeled green bananas, then backed away, fanning herself with the flat of her hand.   The children would be home from school soon. She heard the jeep pull in and stop beside the house. Her father was back early. She knew as soon as she heard him coughing and muttering that he'd been drinking. He snarled and kicked at one of the chickens, and it scurried, clacking, into the bushes. I wish, panic rising like the perpetual heartburn, making her gag, I wish I could disappear.

"Where the hell's my food!"

"Its not ready yet. I didn't expect you until later."

"So you think I should be out working in this hell-heat? Stupid girl. Look at you! What a mess!"

Think of a knife, she told herself slowly. Imagine a knife gutting him like a codfish that comes flattened, stiff, spread open, crusted with salt, packed in boxes. You rip the spines out with the edge of a blade. Her eyes went flat, trying to reflect nothing at all for his fury to latch onto. Once, when her belly was first showing, he had seen something stir in her eye and slammed her hard against the wall, making her teeth crack against each other. Her ribs had ached for days. He had tried to hit her in the stomach, but she'd curled herself tight, and spitting curses he'd gone back out, and come back too drunk for trouble.

Her father sat down on the vinyl couch and stared at the flickering screen where two lovers were kissing passionately. Stay tuned to this channel for more romance, said the announcer. In just a few moments María Estér stars in... and a husky woman's voice whispered, Vivir....Para Ti. To live...for you.

Down the road she could hear the children shouting and wanted to warn them, hush them, but they'd seen the jeep already, and slid into the house hugging books to their chests, and "Bendición, Papi", bless us, they beseeched. He looked them over. "Dios los bendiga y la Virgen" he muttered and turned back to gaze at the screen. Without looking up he told Papo to get out of his school clothes and get down to the plot and help Felo with the planting.

"But Papi..."

"Did you hear me? Don't argue, I'm warning you."

He tried to pull his belt out of his pants, still sitting down. Aurea, the youngest, giggled. He took off his shoe and threw it at her, and she ran to her big sister, clutching at her skirts, and crying "Ay ay ay."

Irritated, Luz pushed the child off her.

"Ay honey, it's too hot."

She smoothed her hair, and told her to stop crying.

"You know it only makes him mad."

While Papo changed into the banana-stained pants he used for farm work, Willie pulled a letter out of one of his schoolbooks and held it out to his father.

"Don Pepe said you forgot to bring the letter home"

"Oh that's right. PAPO!"

Papo came out of the back bedroom the boys shared with their father.

"Léeme esta carta."

Papo took the envelope and said, "Its from Eddie."

"You think you're so smart! Who else would it be from? "

"He says he's working at a new place where they pay better, and if Luz wants she can come stay with them, if she'll help with the children and the house. His wife is pregnant again and gets too tired." There was a small silence, then their father snorted. "A lot of help she'd be!" He ran his eyes over Luz' round body, and she turned away from him toward the stove.

"Then he says next year when I'm fourteen, he could get me some work as an errand boy if I want to come live with him, too." Papo looked up at his father's scowling face and quickly returned to the letter. "And that he knows times are hard here, so if we want to come, tell him a few months ahead and he'll send money for the tickets."

Their father stood up, shouting. "Coño! Does he think a farm runs itself? How the hell can I take care of my parcela if all you brats go running off to Nueva Yor? Your brother's a burro!" He looked around him at the roomful of apprehensive faces. "Papo get the hell down to the parcela and help Felo plant bananas...and don't come back until you finish the first hillside!" Papo went silently out the door. Luz dished up a plate of reheated rice and beans and handed it to Aurea, who carried it carefully across the room to her father. Grumbling and muttering, he settled back onto the sofa and began to eat, gazing blankly at the television screen where the three o'clock novela was starting.

And now...Vivir...Para Ti. The hero, the handsome young painter, was sketching the beautiful wife of the patrón. There were long silences while he worked, and the woman watched him. Luz liked this novela. The young man was falling in love with the patrón's wife, but he was sworn to kill the patrón. Luz couldn't remember why. The young wife didn't love the patrón. Her family was rich and proud, and had forced her to marry him out of ambition. She and the painter went on walks and laughed a lot. Hitching herself up onto a stool by the stove Luz began sopping up the juice from the beans with a piece of bread. It looked like pretty soon something was going to get started between the two of them. She watched absorbedly as the patrón told his young guest that he was going away on business for a few days. Now was their chance.

It was dark when it happened. When she thinks of it she feels the child's small, firm body pressing against the walls of her stomach, and the nausea makes her head spin. Toño had promised to wait every night by the church until she could slip away to see him, and the night Papi went to town to see his brother about something, she'd gone, telling the others she was going to visit her godmother. In case someone checked, she stopped first by her godmother's on the way down.

Several of the neighbors were gathered on the porch. They had talked about the two 'o clock novela, the one with the twin brothers, one good and one bad. The bad one was stealing the good one's sweetheart and they were trying to guess if she would believe his lies or not. Luz thought she wouldn't, but one of the other neighbors said she would, and then she'd find out her mistake and repent.

Luz spent half an hour on the porch, gossiping and sipping coffee. All the time she could feel Toño's cool shadow on the church wall, making her itch with impatience, but her face was placid, and she even asked to see the new embroidery her madrina had just finished. She knew how to hide even her smallest desires. She had always been able to do this, even when she was younger than Aurea.

Finally, she left her madrina's, asking for her blessing, and walked down the road, around the church corner, and straight into Toño's arms. His kisses had suffocated her even then. Even in the cool of the rainy season his hot breath on her face had made her dizzy with the longing to escape. But he smelled good, and he had sweet, dark eyes, and warm brown skin, and when he grazed his lips along her neck, she felt faint with excitement. In fact, his caresses were the only exciting thing that had ever happened. He had pulled her down into the grass, and she had followed him into the wet, green place, burying her face in his shoulder to get away from his lips. She loved his torso. It was the only part of him that didn't try to devour her. The only part she could approach at her own speed. She had placed her palms on his shoulder blades and kept them there until it was over.

When she got home, he was waiting behind the door with the belt in hand and he'd beat her around the house calling her a slut, saying you think I can't see the grass stains on your back? Your mother would get up out of her grave if she knew. I'll teach you to have respect. Then he had dragged her by the hair into the darkened bedroom, thrown her down on the bed, slapped his hard, stained hand over her mouth and done it again.

Think of a knife. The blade ripping the ribs out, leaving him split like this dried fish, leather and salt. She hacked it up and threw it in a pot of water to soak. The baby swam up against her left side, poked a foot or elbow out, sank back into her flesh. Toño was in Connecticut and wrote all the time, through his sister Ana Teresa, but she hadn't answered him. He wanted her to come out and marry him. He knew about the baby from Ana Teresa.

She tried to imagine Connecticut. Rows of fruit trees in straight lines. Barracks with only cold water on an icy morning. Cold like ice cream eaten too fast and sticking in your throat. Cold too cold to touch getting into your skin and bones. Cold enough to wipe out the hot breath smelling of rum that made her vomit, over and over, by the side of the house when he was finished and told her to clean herself up.

Sometimes she thought the baby was Toño's and would smile at her with his same, round freckled mulatto face, and out of sheer relief she would go to Connecticut and live in a tiny room with him and the child. But the nightmare came to her every night, the child with a drunkard's eyes, muddy brown, closed to slits, chewing at her breast, grunting over her in the dark. Her brothers' eyes slid away from her all the time now. Worst of all, what if the child looked like her and she grew to love him, not knowing, until one day her father stood out stark as lightening and she had to rip the boy out of her heart by a hundred tiny sucking roots.

He was whistling as he walked up the dirt road. He had planted a hillside of new bananas, and worked up an appetite. The sun was still cool, just barely warming the moist chill of the early air. As he turned toward the house he met the children going to school. Willie was acting the fool, balancing his book bag on his head. They hesitated when they saw him and he grinned.

"If that thing falls in the mud, you'll have to do all that "spiki eenglich" stuff again." Willie grinned back.

"No, Papi, I'll show Mr. Luna the muddy paper. He won't care."

"Bueno, you better run to school now, because you have Mr. Perez first and he'll smack your behind if you're late. Corre."

"Bendición, Papi" They yelled over their shoulders as they ran.

"Dios los bendiga", God bless you, he called after them. That Willie was a real clown.

He stamped his feet to loosen the mud, scraped it with a stick and went in to breakfast. Luz had made surullos. She brought him a plate full, little fat cigars of cornmeal, fried crisp on the outside, moist and delicious inside. "They're good. You're getting to be as good a cook as your mother." Luz flushed a little at the compliment. "Titi Celita teaches me a little, and madrina." "That's good. When you marry, your husband will always be home for meals."

The comment was meant to be jovial, friendly, but the heaviness of her step moving around the kitchen made it fall flat. Silence fell between them again. He looked away from her, out the door where the chickens carried on their perpetual brooding search for food. He crumbled one of the surullos and threw the pieces out the door. In a moment it was covered by tiny scurrying black and white chicks, cheeping excitedly between the legs of the stolid hens.

Cooking beans, feeding chickens, fetching water, buying fish, washing clothes, making coffee, cutting bananas, sharpening the knife. One afternoon she got back from the store and Aurea handed her a note.

Querida Hermana Luz:

Nos fuimos a nueba Yor pa bibir con Eddie. Aquí ya no ce puede bibir. El nos mandó el pasaje, por eso tubimos que ir al pueblo el otro dia a recojerlo. No dijimo na pa que papi no supiera. que nos mata si llega a saber. Aquí ya no ce bibe. Dios te cuide y te guarde como dice madrina y que todo salga bien. Se despiden tus hermanos que te quieren.

Papo y Willie

[Dear Sister Luz: We went to nueba Yor to live with Eddie. This is no life here. He sent us the tikets thats why we had to go to town the other day to get them. We didn't say nothing to Papi so he woodn't no. cuz he'd kill us if he new. This is no life. God bless and protec you like madrina says and that everything comes out OK. Goodbye from your brothers who love you. Papo and Willie]

Spell out the words of the scrawled note. Scrub the iron pot with a fistful of steel wool. Grip the table against the pain of that goodbye. Nothing but a dullness left. Fetch water. Cook beans. Cut bread. Papo had always been her favorite, since she had brought him to sleep close to her after their mother's death. Aurea had been a newborn baby so her aunt Celita had taken her home for awhile, but Papo, who was one and a half at the time, had crept in each night to sleep curled against her ribs. With the boys gone, it was so lonely that some days it was hard to breathe. One of those aching, monotonous mornings, she decided suddenly she would name the child Papo for that same caress of the ribs it gave her, and she felt the first stirring of a small, stubborn love.

Late in the night he came home, staggering a little, up the narrow road from the store where he had spent the evening buying twenty-five cent shots of rum. A little rum made him want to fight, to give one of the kids a good whipping for lacking respect. A little rum made him mad. But a lot of rum made his heart turn to water.

It was very late. The moon had drenched the red soil with shadows. It looked almost purple. The small house was dark. He stepped toward it out of the darkness of the trees and blinked in the sudden light. Swaying a little, he stood looking at the shuttered windows. They gave the house a stupid, closed look, like a sleeping child. He pulled back, slipping on the wet ground, and caught at the heavy bushes that showered him with cold drops of water.

The air would be stuffy and still behind those shutters. Nothing had moved in the house since Ofelia had died. Now that the last of his sons were gone to the North, the house would be even quieter. His thoughts shied away from Luz, her swelling body. Shied and were pulled back. He had an image of Ofelia at sixteen, pregnant with their first child, her arms like smooth brown cream, her laughing face. She had been thin and faded at the end, but it had taken two of her brothers and his own sister Celita to pull him away from her body.

Some night bird dipped across the white air with a hoarse cry. Startled, his foot slid on the slick ground. He grabbed for Pancho, but Pancho had gone home, so he threw his arm around the limb of a tree to steady himself, then sagged against its rigid shoulder, and sobbed drunkenly. Across the gap of light, his house stood shuttered against him. Ofelia was buried. His sons were gone. He was afraid of Luz, with her growing heaviness and her silence. He was afraid of the still house where his daughters slept in the wooden dark, with their arms around each other. After a while he stumbled over to the jeep, crawled into the back and slumped into a heavy sleep.

The rain fell so hard from the sky that it bounced halfway back again, and there was more water than air between the wet houses with their sodden planks of wood. Papi sat snarling at the television, and the humidity made the plastic sofa stick to his shirt back.

When Aurea sidled out of the bedroom his eyes followed her. Está hecha una mujercita. Soon the neighborhood boys would be following her around.

"Ven acá." he barked.

Startled, she obeyed.

"Do any of the boys bother you?"

"No, Papi" She sounded puzzled.

"I better not hear about you going off with any boys and fooling around. You walk straight home from school, you hear me?"

"Si, Papi."

"Dame un beso."

She looked at him.

"I'm your father and I said give me a kiss. You don't have any respect." Timidly she bent and pecked at his cheek.

He chuckled, held her chin with his rough fingers and planted mouthful of rum and cigarette fumes in a sloppy kiss on her lips. Aurea stood up, watching him with frightened eyes. He slapped at her behind.

"Vete y ayuda a tu hermana. Go on. Go help your sister. "

He glanced up and saw Luz in the kitchen doorway, looking as stiff and hard as a stick of firewood.

"Vente Aurea. Help me wash the dishes."

That afternoon the two daughters sat behind the house under the overhanging tin roof, scrubbing the stains from their father's pants. Their hands went round and round on the soapy cloth, grinding at the dirt with their sore knuckles. Slowly the water turned muddier and muddier. After a while the sun came out, and it got hot again. When they were finished, Luz wrung the pants out and hung them on a bush to dry, then she poured the dirty water out onto the steaming ground. In the late yellow light it seemed to smoke there for a while, before it soaked into the red earth.

It had happened. The young wife and the painter had become lovers. Madrina was scandalized. Luz' neighbor said it was only natural, with the patrón so old and mean, but madrina said it taught women bad habits. Luz went over to madrina's to watch. Her Aunt Celita was up at the house doing the cooking and had sent her for some of madrina's oregano, telling her to take her time.

The wife had decided that she couldn't live in that house anymore, and she was going. Luz watched, wide eyed, as the rich young woman stuffed her jewelry into her purse and hurriedly packed a bag. Suddenly a door opened and one of the servants came in and stared at the wife's suitcase. "Ay, Dios mío" gasped madrina, "now she's caught for sure." But the servant just said "God bless you, señora". There were only two minutes left of the episode. The young wife looked around her beautiful home one more time, and then went out, closing the door behind her.

Luz and her madrina and the neighbor all let out their breath.

"Well I hope she makes it", said the neighbor. "She deserves something better than that ugly old man."

"Hush, Luisa" said madrina. "She shouldn't have married him if she wasn't going to be faithful."

"Ay mija, it isn't always that simple. She hadn't met the painter then."

Luz kissed her godmother and left. She could hear the women arguing as she walked slowly back up the hill.

Dear Toño.

God grant that this letter finds you well, as thank God it leaves me.
This is to tell you that I am coming I am bringing Aurea because I
can't leave her here alone with Papi the boys have gone north. We are
coming Monday morning the eleventh. Ana Teresa got the ticket for
me. Papi doesn't know anything.

Your sincere friend,

Luz

She dressed Aurea in the bedroom. In each of her shoes was a
twenty dollar bill stolen from Papi's pants. She tied their mother's
wedding and engagement rings on a ribbon Ana Teresa had given
her from her cousin's graduation, and hung it around Aurea's neck,
tucking it down under her collar so it wouldn't show. The tickets
were folded up and pinned to the inside of her own blouse. Their
father breathed heavily in the next room. Nothing would wake him
now. Not for hours.

Last night she'd slipped out for a minute and hidden a plastic shopping bag of clothing for the two of them under an old rusted out car
that had sat at the edge of the road for fifteen years and six months.
She knew exactly because Doña Luisa said some drunken idiot had
driven it off the bank the same night Papi had driven her mother to
the hospital in labor with her. Luisa had run out, afraid her pregnant
friend had been hurt. "It sounded like his car, you know. If your
father had been a single man I would have stayed in my kitchen and
said God's will be done, but I really loved your mother, honey, and
I was worried about her, since it was Saturday and I knew her pains

had started. But when I went out it was some other drunk fool. The car was completely wrecked, so he just left it there and no-one's figured out how to move it since. Way up here, it'd cost a fortune to have it towed to the dump in Yagrumo."

Yesterday she had stopped Mundín on his way back from the last run to town and asked him to pick her up by the church, an hour before Mass. "We're going to Ponce. Aurea has bad dreams. About Mami. I'm taking her to a lady who interprets them."

Luz knew Mundín was an espiritista. He'd nodded knowingly.

"I haven't told Papi, because he doesn't believe in that. He thinks we're going to see Titi Celita in Yagrumo." She had looked at him anxiously.

"Your father is going to get a big surprise when he dies, that's all. I won't say a word to him, mija. You're a good girl to take care of your sister like that."

* * * * *

It was colder than she could imagine, even after all these months. The bus was always late. She was grateful for the small tropical sun that burned in her huge belly, but her hands turned red, then blue, and her lips got tiny cracks in them, that stung when Toño kissed her.

It had been the ugliness that hurt when she first got off the plane, clutching Aurea's hand from the terror of that landing. The rows and rows of brown brick buildings with scrawny little trees here and there. She couldn't understand how people could live like that. Toño had been glad to see her. He'd kept patting her belly, and grinning, and trying to kiss her face in public, which made her uncomfortable. He'd been nice to Aurea, too, rumpling her hair and calling her little sister. He'd even stayed home the first few days, helping her get settled into the tiny one-bedroom apartment. It was as big as the house back home, but with no land around it, the rooms seemed cramped and airless. But she made the best of it, hanging her and Aurea's clothes in the little closet with Toño's shirts, stashing their underwear in a cardboard box under the bed. That's where she hid her money, too, under a flap of the cardboard box.

He hadn't let her take the job in the restaurant down the street, saying his woman had no need to work. But he was gone from late morning until late at night, so she took care of the neighbors' children and did a little sewing. After a while she made a few friends in the neighborhood, and it was one of them, a Dominican woman, who got her the housecleaning job. Slowly the crumpled bills accumulated.

In case he heard about her absences, she told Toño about her Dominican friend. Since he came home so late, she said, she liked to eat over there sometimes. For the company. At first Aurea went with her to her cleaning job and helped, but the señora didn't like it, and after a while Aurea went straight to the Dominicana's house to watch TV and wait for Luz.

There it was. The bus pulled up, hot, stinking, full of people hanging from the metal bar like clothes on a clothesline. She hauled herself up, trying to move fast, but as soon as she got onto the first step, the bus driver closed the door and lurched forward. She fell against the wall and hung on as hard as she could, then she felt a deep twisting pain in her belly. She moaned, and gripped the rail so hard her fingers went white. A black woman in the first seat took one look at her and yelled, "Stop the damn bus. This girl's in labor".

"Oh, shit!" The driver turned to look at her as he pulled over. "Can't you people do anything right?"

"How often are your contractions, hon?....HOW OFTEN..uuhh... Kay Mucho?"

"No onderstan Inglich"

"Hey Sandy, send García up. Make it fast."

Once as a child, she had been at her aunt's house near the beach during a hurricane. Huddling in the Lion's Club, which was the strongest building around, she had seen the waves pick up pieces of wood and throw them into the air. She was the wave. She was the wood. Each time a wave hit, she felt herself flying up and out, into a thousand pieces. At first there were quiet spells where she floated, eyes closed, listening to the foreign voices speaking to each other around her bed, but after a while there was only the storm. At last she felt herself splitting open, her skin ripping like the peel of a mango torn to expose the dripping flesh. Then something slippery, hairy, hard-and-soft like a mango, pushed itself from her raw body and slithered onto the table.

"It's a girl. Tell her it's a little girl"

"Tienes una nena."

Fearfully, she looked down. The tiny face was the color of coffee with too much milk. She was waterlogged and swollen from the storm, and looked like no-one Luz had ever seen before, but her hands were like tiny, perfect hermit crabs, clawing at the air.

That was all. There was not a single clue. The child's skin was like Luz' dead mother's, a creamy brown. She went over and over each miniature detail. The eyes, the chin, the wet black hair. She touched the crinkled mouth with her fingertip and the lips curled back like an opening bud of hibiscus, and then closed again, sucking tight. Luz watched in amazement. The child was new, as if she had been born that minute from the waves. Not one of them had left his mark on her. Looking down at the little cream face, she remembered the girl on the novela, the one who married the good twin. She had finally found out who her real father was, a kind old doctor who had been looking for her for years. No one would be looking for this daughter. No one had the answer.

The nurse held the dark, wet head to Luz' breast and after a moment the pink tongue touched her nipple and the tiny mouth fastened itself onto her. Images drifted through her mind: a baby goat, a limpet clinging tight to a surf-washed rock. A shell found at the beach by her aunt's house after the big storm, pale brown and white on the outside, glowing smooth pink inside. A secret between her and the sea.

"What's her name, honey?"

"My neing ees Luz Rodriguez"

"No, no, the baby...uh...Too Bay-bay"

She stared at the nurse for a moment.

Luz y mar. Mar y Luz.

"Ponle Mariluz," she said. "Herr neing ees Mariluz."

She took the pencil from the nurse and wrote it down in a firm round hand.

The nurses were finally gone, and her baby drowsed across her belly, still latched on, sleepily pulling thin threads of milk from Luz' swollen breasts. The other bed in the room was empty, so it was quiet, the hospital noises muffled by the thick door. She closed her eyes and imagined hearing a rooster crowing in the late night stillness. She still wasn't used to the night time here, noisy and unnaturally quiet at the same time, with its grumbling traffic, but no tree frogs, or crickets, or dogs.

Toño had been and gone, storming out into the snow. Probably for good. Once he had been the only pleasure in her life. She was sorry to see him go, but not sad. She had train fare to New York, and Eddie and his wife were expecting her.

"Why didn't you wait for me, before you named her?" he'd asked. She had taken a deep breath, as deep as she could with the stitches burning and aching.

"She's not your child, Toño."

"WHAT! "

"She's not your baby."

"Coño! Now you tell me? All this time living in my house and now you tell me its not my baby?" He had raged up and down the room. Threatened to hit her, called her a cheat, a slut, a bad woman who had ruined his life. Cried because she wasn't his woman after all. Luz had watched him without blinking.

Was it Cheito's? Luis'? Miguel's? She shook her head tiredly.

"Who the hell's is it then?"

"Mine, Toño, no-one else's"

"What are you? La Virgen María? ¡No jodes! Whose is it?"

"Mine"

She lay back on the pillows and thought of that last morning in the silent house, her father still snoring, sprawled across his bed. She had sharpened the knife til it gleamed even in the dark. It was like a razor blade, humming to her quiet breathing. She had stood looking down on him for a moment, the blade trembling in her hand. Then she had laid that thin, bitter steel on the pillow next to his face, so it would be the first thing he saw when he woke.

First Snow

For Robin Sterns, 1953-1972

I never knew you in a season of green leaves and flowers. When we met it was early gold in New England, and the first frost of September had just touched the last thick grasses of August. Five years in this country, and I had never yet loved a piece of land. I'd come straight from the lush tropical forests of a Caribbean mountain range to the South Side of Chicago, a landscape that hurt my senses, and although Lake Michigan's steely windblown waters sometimes won my grudging admiration, though I stood still to watch the smoggy, prune-colored skies bruise into color at sunset, there was nothing that tempted me to root. That summer I decided to leave before another sooty winter clamped down on the city. At the last minute I got into a small college in the White Mountains of New Hampshire that was within my means and an easy hitchhike from my boyfriend's school in Vermont. All I wanted was out.

Riding the bus north from Boston we swung through the dark, following a thread of lights, stopping to let silent passengers off in front of small town post offices and supermarkets. Untalkative women and men and sleepy children stepped out into the leafy smelling dark and the bus ground back onto I-93, while the land rose in ever sharper granite shadows out of reach of the headlights. You came the other way—the bus from White River Junction that meets the New York train.

That first night they put us all at the Inn until the dorms were ready. Your tentative knock came just as I was pulling out a nightgown, trying to settle down from the strange thrill of being a thousand miles from home. "Oh, God", I thought, "a debutante. What on earth are we going to talk about?" You looked like a model, and I was horrified to discover that you were one. Tall, thin, a head covered with true-gold hair the exact color of the looted Egyptian treasures at the Oriental Institute, big blue eyes and a touch of Texas in your soft voice. I was fresh from the rallies over Cambodia, fresh from discussing the myth of vaginal orgasm and the politics of housework. I wore old mauve lace and flowered cotton dresses from second hand stores one day, lumberjack shirts and painter's pants the next, my rarely brushed hair hanging in dark tangles around my face. "Oh well," I thought, "It's just for the night."

But in the morning it was a new world. The roads we had barreled down in the dark were lined with the pale yellow and shocking white of thick-standing birch trees whose peeling skin revealed glimpses of smooth touchable pinks and creamy oranges. A glittering frost had spread its net over the landscape, each blade and stalk of grass outlined in winking, shifting flashes of light; acres of sparkling beauty without iron gates and railings, without parking meters or fire hydrants. And just down the road a swift shallow river sang between a bed of brown pebbles and the thinnest possible layer of green translucent ice. Equally new to northern seasons, we were unanimous in our exhilaration.

From first frost to snowfall we were drunk with glory. The college administration made us roommates, and we became inseparable. Neither of us was quite what we had seemed. You had a wild, manic sense of humor, and an iron tang that your easy curls and winsome charm made surprising, while I was much shyer than my stride. I showed you my poems, scratched in green ink into my journal, and you took them to heart, probing them, tasting the words, asking intently after each scrap of meaning. You played me your favorite rock bands with that same intentness..."You see? You hear that? There! That!" until I had satisfied your urgency to share the one beat you loved best.

We filled our room with the litter of the shedding trees, each new magenta or salmon leaf as astonishing as the last. In your long grey coat you walked in the flaming woods for hours, coming back silent, full of autumn, the season neither of us had ever seen before. And you waited for snow. Growing up in Houston, and this last year in Israel, you had never seen it fall. You wanted to be outside when it began, you said, (like girls planning their first embraces), to see the first flakes spinning down and lift your face to the kiss of winter.

Meanwhile we told stories, talking from bed to bed in the dark. I remember your face in the lamplight, soft and hard, telling me about your father's affairs with girls your age, your mother's ambitions for you, your unripened ovaries that let you forget about birth control, all the stupid things men said in order to bed you. Your misfortune in looking like Goldilocks.

I lent you books. You drew me pictures. Our lives began to knit together, like the matted roots of wildflowers, blooming in the narrow openings of the forest. Nights while the stars swung overhead we leaned in slow, delicious free fall toward each other's arms, knowing we would arrive in our own good time. Apples, berries, nuts, pumpkins, late corn all spilled their abundance from the roadside stands. Around us the trees glowed in the colors of sun-ripe fruit, flickering and bright as faces turned to a hidden fire. But all the time the roots were reaching for a place deeper than the approaching frost, a race against the tilt of the earth's axis.

David still came every other weekend. Whenever he arrived, you whisked yourself out of sight and went to stay with a friend, pushing privacy on us just a little too soon, ruining the tact of your exit with a wry and hilarious wink, your falsetto voice drifting back to us over your shoulder as you waltzed across the empty fields singing "Roooooses, Oh, Roooses and Moooonlight!".

I dream sometimes of catching you as you run, crying Robin, don't go, come back, with your saucy, tea-cup-blue eyes full of maple leaves. Stay here, with your bad dreams from the forced sale of your girlhood to modeling agents who fingered you while your mother took the cash saying that's the price of glamour. Come back with your hair of Jerusalem gold and your monkey screeches in the dark, and give me time to leave him for you. But you turn, laughing, and wave, and leave me here among the living.

Ten years later and a thousand miles west of the place where I first heard the news, I wake with the same muscle spasm freezing my neck. This grey, blizzard-ridden morning in the Midwest, I can still imagine you as I did all the first winter of your absence, walking toward me through the snow-choked forests, on endless pilgrimage back to me, to life, to the lighted windows of our house. "It took me weeks to get here," you would say, coming in and stamping the snow from your boots, "months, years, it took me ten years to get here, but I had to let you know I was alright. It wasn't me in the car. It was someone else."

Like you, I was asleep when it happened, or I would have felt you tear away. I woke from a deep, dreamless dark to find David bending over me, and your note, "Gone to Maine for the weekend with Mary and Jeff. Back Sunday night. I love you." Then I was in the kitchen, stooping to take the soufflé out of the oven. Sorry I had missed your departure. Looking forward to food. I had the casserole in my hands, just setting it on the counter, when they came in together, the three of them, solemn as storks stepping through the door. "I wanted to tell you because you're her friend," he said, and I thought

Robin, you've been annoying the Dean again. Now he's angry, you and your jokes. But why tell *me*? "Robin and Jeff were killed," he said, "in an accident two hours ago in Maine."

Wait a minute. What? What did you say? Wait a minute. My mind stuttering, trying to catch up with my body, which was already clinging to David and sobbing so hard that when the others ran in, I couldn't even say your name.

Nothing was real, except once I remember Beverly's shocked face in my doorway saying, "Their things are still in their rooms!" It made no sense. That, and the way my mind went in circles, wondering where the hell you were when I needed you because, Robin, something terrible happened, and then remembering, each time with a slightly smaller sickening jolt, that the terrible thing and your absence were the same. On your wall was a postcard with a painting of the Snow Queen, white and bloodless on her silver sleigh, driving away into the blizzard with young Hans, bound by cruel enchantments, clinging to the back. I lay and watched it for hours, waiting for you to come home.

Much later, when she could talk again, Mary told me how it was. You were dozing, your head cushioned against the door. Jeff was driving, and she sat between you. She said the car slid outward into the curve and she turned to Jeff and said "we're going to hit that truck," and his last words were "I know," and then she was lying on the road watching the reflection of red flashing lights on the wet tar. They lifted her into an ambulance, and put Jeff beside her. She kept asking where you were, and they'd tell her you were being taken care of, and she would know from their voices, but she kept on asking anyway, over and over. Your body was lying sideways across the edge of the road where it was flung after you flew away. Do you remember? Your head was like a coconut shell the boys throw on the rocks, shattered and leaking.

You were shipped back to Texas, your head bandaged together for burial, your black Gaza dress with the winking mirrors eased onto your body. You were put away into the ground and I never saw you again. Nothing was real.

That night, after they told me, I went outside to breathe, to cross the dark field to our friends, to find one last molecule of you. I couldn't believe your warm mouth would not cross the final gap to mine. But when I stepped off the porch and looked up, the stars were gone. Soft cold feathers brushed against my cheeks. It had come at last. The first snowfall of winter. Huge, slow flakes spinning lazily down like a silent drift of flowers, settling on the dry branches, filling the ruts in the road, covering the last red leaves in a blanket of white, hiding the path and falling endlessly, for heartbreaking months on end, out of the low grey sky.

Spring was a long time coming that year. I wrote and wrote and wrote, while the snow landed its powdery blows bruise after bruise, and the cold made the roads heave up and the stones crack. Grief and winter gripped my body and opened me, while I sat at my desk without you, sinking my first deep roots into North America. I forced the icy sap to flow in my veins, cold as the rivers that fall from the Presidentials. I listened to the branches breaking under their own frozen weight and refused to break. I watched the sputtering of the northern lights over the empty road of leafless trees, and rose from my bed to fill trackless sheets of paper. I drank with small, hungry wild things at frozen pools, and gnawed the astringent needles of pine for their tangy taste of endurance.

And one day the roots went deep enough. It would be too much to say I forgave the universe your death, but when I bent to look at the blunt elbows of crocuses, shoving their way into the air, and saw the sun calling dry sticks into swollen bud, I called them good. I learned that wild cherries bloom deep in the forest where nobody sees them, that humans don't matter to the tender sap-filled wood. Twigs swelled like young breasts, and unfurled in a thousand fans of pale green. Never in all my years of tropical profusion had I seen blossom break out of silence like this. Ice cracked from the shore and was swept away on leaping waters.

One night in the middle of our friendship you told me about your trip into the Sinai. Leaping off the bed you showed me how, con-vinced of miracles, you struck at the rocks with your stick again and again, certain of water. You said you knew exactly how it would taste. You held the stones in your hand, hefting them, measuring their weight, joyfully cracking the stick of your aliveness against their rough sides.

I have outlived you so long now, your ghost could be my daughter. That winter as you walked the starry road away from us I learned perseverance, and this has been my reward. Even here, facing the hard rock of despair that blocks my way, in the most barren places I hear it: the trickling of water, sweet and sharp as the first wild strawberries, that spring after they buried you. It is always with me, coaxing the words from my tongue. Sometimes it breaks my heart with thirst, sometimes it runs into the cup of my palms, the miracle of those who endure, the ice cold water of hope in the desert where you left me, to find my own way home.

Last Rites

"I'm calling Hospice," Rosa said to the back of Paul's head. She thought he wasn't going to answer but he nodded, once, without turning. He was dying. She'd known it for months. He no longer denied it.

She stood staring at the pattern of his disarranged hair, pushed this way and that by all those hours on his pillow, little tufts sticking out wantonly, playfully, near the top of his head. Ridiculous looking hair is not the sort of thing you associate with death.

She knew she should feel tender, sad. She should be attentive, caring, suppressing her wishes and feelings to ensure him the best time she could manage in the worst six months of his life. But all she could do was stand and stare at his sticking-out hair and will him to turn around and say something to her, anything.

She clenched her jaw to keep inside the words that were already in her mouth itching to get said. They slithered between her teeth and came hissing out: "Say something."

He didn't. He sat immobile and stared out the window at the obscenely sunny day. May first. Ironic. Two days before his fifty-fourth birthday. Jesus. He averted his eyes from his neglected garden and watched the little girl next door playing with her new puppy. She cuddled it like a doll, only the pup wriggled and got away. Did she know he was next door dying? Would she be sorry?

Rosa didn't look sorry, just pissed all the time. As if it was her tragedy and not his. He should be the one to be furious. But he wasn't. He felt ... what? He thought about it, trying something he'd never practiced much. Sad? Sort of. Scared? A little. What he felt most was—what was the word?—resigned? Probably. The world was shitting on Paul Amarco and there was nothing he could do about it. There was nothing at all to do except take those pills, eat when he could manage it, sleep when the pain let up some, and sit, while he still could, and stare at the puppy scampering out there, at the little girl, the grass, the sunshine. That sunshine.

Rosa banged the phone on its cradle. Banged the pots on the stove. Slammed the cupboard doors. It wasn't fair. She felt cheated. Now it could never be different. When did he stop being the man she fell in love with? He wasn't like that when they met. His silences crept in so slowly she was used to them before she realized how unhappy she felt. He just talked less and less. She felt lonelier when he was around that when he wasn't. When she talked to him she felt like a radio beaming out one sided conversation, like a one woman show.

True, he was accommodating, went along with all her plans. Her sister envied her the ease with which she got her way. "You have no idea what it's like, she said, we can't move a chair without a fight." But Rosa thought he would accept anything rather than give an opinion or heaven forbid, state a wish. As to his feelings ... well! If she didn't know better she would have thought he had none- except one- the one feeling he was open about was his love for her. He told her so and he touched her constantly, her hair, her arm, her leg, her breast, as if he nourished himself with the feel of her. She would have left if it hadn't been for that. She almost left anyway. But in March she got him to agree, God that took work, got him to agree to go with her to a therapist. Just once. He was no doubt afraid the man would worm some trivial preference out of him and blow his cover.

But it was not to be. His doctor ordered that bunch of tests. One moment Paul was a vigorous young man—middle-aged, but young—and the next he was dying. Who goes to a marriage counselor when he's dying?

She set the bowl down carefully so she wouldn't bang it. The soup smelled delicious. She'd loaded it with every tender nourishing vegetable she could find, the first expensive early peas, asparagus, dandelion greens. He would eat only a drop. She banged the soup spoon. She stood staring at the loaded tray. "Sometimes" she said to it, "sometimes I think he got himself sick with cancer so he wouldn't have to go to the therapist."

Paul disapproved of Rosa's behavior. She was acting like a sulky teenager. Had been since that god awful day at the doctors office. But after that first appointment with the hospice people, she really lost it. They'd made plans for his dying. He shook his head at the absurdity of it. Plans! But what happened next had not been in the plan. After the woman left, Rosa asked what he felt. What could he feel? He'd hardly begun to lift his shoulders in a shrug before she shot out another stupid question, what did he think? And when he didn't answer her, she yelled. Rosa never yelled. Oh, they had their fights. But yell? Never. He couldn't stand yelling—and she kept on asking questions, crying, screaming, telling him he had to talk to her. Was she supposed to live with a corpse? She said that. To him, lying on his deathbed, a man dying of cancer. And she said if he was going to lie there and act dead he might as well die now and get it over.

He could only stare at her. What in heaven's name was happening to Rosa? He could only think the strain had mentally unhinged her. What she did next, he still could hardly believe it, was pick up his water glass from his bedside table, the water for his medicines, and throw it across the room. Miraculously it didn't shatter, just bounced and left a trail of water on the floor and along the foot of his hospital bed. He shifted his stare to the dark streak marring the smooth tan lightweight blanket.

Over the days, then weeks, his astonishment slowly gave way to irritation. She might be horribly frightened or crazy with grief but he was the one dying. She nursed him and fed him but she railed against him all the time. She gave him no peace. It was what he wanted, peace, to lie there or sit by the window and think about the injustice of his early death. He was young still. He was owed years more. Instead he was in pain and it would get worse he knew. He wanted her solicitude, her kindness, not just soup and clean sheets. He wanted to withdraw from the racket of the life that was being denied him. He wanted quiet. The irritation grew. He knew all too well what he was feeling now.

Meanwhile Rosa sputtered and spat out vituperation in a trance. It no longer burst out of her like firecrackers lit by spontaneous generation. It was more a kind of terminal stubbornness born out of desperation. It was her last six months too.

Alongside the obstinately raging Rosa there was another Rosa standing or walking beside her wherever she went. This Rosa was wide-eyed, shocked, amazed. "How could you?" she would whisper. "How could you ? What is this you are doing? Are you out of your mind?" There were two Rosas thanking the hospice volunteer who stayed with Paul while they shopped, two Rosas sitting at the café having a cup of coffee, or stopping at the library for a book to read at bedtime, for another to read to Paul when he had enough attention available.

That was in the daytime. At night, alone in their old bed, she tossed and turned and almost drowned in tidal waves of sorrow and loss. At night after a day of storms of fury, she wept.

It was in July, maybe August—Rosa wasn't sure—that Paul began to change. She was talking to him, the way she always did now, snapping the words out, sharp, sarcastic. He was hunching down in his chair by the window, his pajamas loose on his thinning body. If he'd had a corner of him that still doubted the doctor's prognosis, it must be gone now—he was very sick. He muttered something. She wasn't sure she heard right. The next time he said it there was no mistaking. He said "bitch!".

That was all for a while, the occasional muttered "bitch". And then, one day, all of a sudden, the great and god awful champagne cork he kept his gullet stoppered with popped out, and words frothed out of him. He told her, then told her again, what he thought about how she was behaving. He cursed her for an unfeeling cow, for a loud-mouthed, self-centered pig. She fought back, yell for yell, insult for insult, blaming him for all her pent-up rage and sorrow, all the pain she felt from his silences, his withdrawals. He defended himself. At length. Lord knows where he got the energy from.

It was bizarre. He was truly unpleasant now, resentful, complaining, quarrelsome, but she was often happy. And full of hope. The spirit rising in him like sap brought color to his face. Surely he could not die now.

One day, in a quiet spell between fights, while he stared at what passed for a meal those days—he hardly ate—he said, out of no-where, "She killed herself." Rosa knew immediately he meant his mother. Paul had always said, his whole family said, it was an ac-cident. Not an accident? Rosa stared blankly at his contorted face. "She wanted to die. I knew she did. She never tried to hide it. Why, Rosa? Why?" And he cried, the large, slow tears moving down his cheeks, the first she had ever seen. She didn't move or say anything, afraid to interrupt what was happening.

And that night he told her about his mother's silences and for the first time listened to Rosa's pain at his refusal to speak. He lay, and she sat, quietly and companionably for a long time until he fell asleep.

Two days later when she was telling him how she had finally planted and mulched the shrub she'd bought for his birthday months back, a rare soft pink azalea he'd considered too expensive to buy for himself, he asked what she would do when he died. "Smash things!", she said, and burst into tears. For the first time she sobbed out her sorrow in his arms.

They lived now in a torrent of strife broken by small intimate truces. He spent his waking hours rehearsing what to say next, waiting for her to come back into the room to dispute or contradict and more and more frequently, to tell her what he felt, the anger, the grief at his life curtailed. The emptiness of no future. They cried together then. And sometimes, in the middle of his ever more frequent drugged sleeps, a quivering sensation woke him, a feeling he tentatively, reluctantly, identified as joy. He was in pain, he was dying. How could he feel joy? Soon he began to feel a stir of hope. How could he die when he felt so alive?

But he did, on a morning in October, with Rosa lying at his side, her arms around him on the narrow bed. He smiled one small, last smile and whispered, "Don't ... smash.. the azaleas".

Y Tuesta El Sol

My hair curls in Puerto Rico, rolls right up in the tropical humidity like spaghetti on a fork. Small tufts and ends stick out here and there in a carefree fashion all over my head. Some part of me has to be carefree. I'm here because my mother has broken her collarbone the way the aged with thinned bones do. She's in a hospital complaining about the nurses, the doctors, her sisters, her neighbors, her daughters and the pain. My father is at home, not clear where his wife has gone, not clear that I am his daughter and not my mother come back as mysteriously as she has left. As the light slants in the afternoon, he becomes anxious, herds Dick and me indoors, locks gates, locks doors, closes us into the hot, humid, dark, mosquito-filled, air behind the jalousies.

I leave him every day, by lying about where I'm going (To the store, Papi. I'll bring you back some cake.) Or sneaking past him to the car. The neighbors watch out for him, send him food he won't touch. He eats cake and cookies mostly, which he says are "suave", smooth, easy to digest, the most nutritious food. And then with my husband Dick at the wheel, at my side, I trek this Medicaid-less landscape from small dark dismal old-age home to unsuitable, unthinkable nursing home all over Bayamón and out beyond.

We find the places we finally choose sooner than this sounds only I don't realize it. I need to search and search. Most are ordinary, drab, small one-story suburban cement houses cut up into cubicles, locked fore and aft, housing fifteen patients. And managers. And staff. I've never experienced this kind of institutional squalor before, or dementia en masse, or so many drugged old people. And I visit the hospital every day, return to my father every day. There are traffic jams, a heat wave. And fear, my fear, of responsibility over adults, over these particular adults and of the violence always threatening between my parents now. The absolute necessity of keeping them apart while my mother recovers and probably long after that. My mother is tinder after years locked up with my progressively more confused and irresponsible father, after changes in her I only now reluctantly admit. They stand bone naked now, all the soft conformity to social norms, all the politeness and pretense stripped from them. At last Dick sees what he's only heard about in stories I tell about my childhood, of my mother's petty meanness, of my father's irrational tyrannies. Waves of the mortal terror I have always felt around my parents sweep over me: the fear of ever again having my life at their mercies in any way.

Nothing I have heard or read or experienced prepares me for this journey on a sea of fear, guilt, concern, sorrow. Guilt for not instantly taking her home to Cambridge with me or for not moving to Puerto Rico and giving my life to her care as my mother wants but never quite says. And oh, the sorrow. Not only for what is happening to them - taken from their home, from their independence, their adulthood. The sorrow is also for me because for the first time in my life I am fatherless and motherless. Tears spill from me without sound as I force myself to see that I cannot, must not, wait to consult my mother, that that kind of respect (or cravenness) has already pushed her past her limit, that I need now, probably needed long before, to simply move in and take over, override their stated wishes. I could have saved them the malnutrition, spared them each other's violence, rescued them from their self-imposed penury and spent their money for them willy-nilly.

I didn't want to. I do not want to now. I, who most emphatically never want to parent anyone or anything anymore, just barely exempting my dog, am parenting my parents now, moving them about as arbitrarily as I once shifted my children. "We're moving to Chicago, my dears. You're sure to like it." They didn't.

My parents don't. My mother says she does and then asks to be taken home to heal. My father stands at the gate of the spacious institution I found for him and asks the way home. They don't want to be where they are. They may never want to be anywhere but home.

Now. Do I sell their house out from under them?

They're eating though, three times a day. For the first time in years my father eats food not cake, my mother is coaxed to take a meal. But that's only a reassurance I recite aloud to myself because the part of me that's sorrowing doesn't care for their bodies, their health, their teeth, their bones. That part of me cares only for their feelings. I, like the good child I was raised to be, am supposed to make my parents feel good no matter what. At fifty-seven I grow up a bit. I make my parents suffer.

"Para que suuufraas..." the old song goes. "So you can suuuuffer". A lover's song of vengeance. Well, I could sing a song of vengeance now, couldn't I, vengeance for the years of suffering as a child from what was, and it becomes clearer as my parents get cleansed of pretense and I retrieve my memories, a pretty crazy household. What I do instead is cry, tears for them, tears for me, now one, now the other, sometimes both.

What, I ask, would be the non-ageist, non-classist, just and generous societal response to a problem like theirs and mine? I wish I had my mind free enough of my own distress, to lay out the myriad possibilities. But I can't think of anything but what I didn't have: a peaceful childhood, with justice, with the absence of fear and violence. The only solution I can think of right now is what I've yearned to do since I could plan, what I secretly and magically worked at while I seemed to be simply raising my children: to remake my childhood, to start over again and do it right this time so that they would be different, and all would have been different, and it would all be different now.

1990

My mother sits on a plastic chair next to my father, leaning over to talk in his ear, raising her voice for one word out of ten so that I wonder how he gets her meaning, which he mostly does. She looks blooming, dressed up and healthy-looking for the first time in several years, since she cracked several bones and I moved her to a nursing home. Her face is rosy with rouge and black-rimmed red earrings make bright spots setting off the black of her dress. Papi looks haggard and old, old, skin drifting into deep sags, deep caves above his slightly clouded eyes, dressed in a muted red shirt and far too short khaki shorts that let a soft, tightly round testicle peep out beside his thigh. When she says playfully into his blank face, again and again. "Quién soy?" ("Who am I?") "Quién soy?" "Ouién soy?" he finally answers "Algo que es mio." ("Something that is mine") and kisses her briefly on the lips. He'd know her if her molecules were dispersed on the ocean floor, and claim her as his own, his private property.

They sit here for a while, Papi pushing the soft chocolate cookies we brought for him into his mouth, leaving cookie smears at the corners and offering some to her, to me, to Dick, telling us how good they are for you. He keeps telling Mami how young and well she looks, "Te ves joven. Que bien te ves." with such approval that she smiles and tosses her head. She is playful, affectionate, sad, and slightly impatient when he doesn't hear or understand. He keeps saying "Vámonos! Vámonos pa' casa," as if he is the one visiting and it's time for him to take her home. He doesn't once respond when she repeats, "No tenemos casa ... We have no home any more."

I want to leave them alone and I want to be here watching my parents, my mother, my father, recognizing them and their relationship unbroken by distance or dementia, the relationship that molded my childhood years and circumscribed my emotional choices. I want to watch this small reconstruction, one small hour, like a dispersed singing-group's reunion concert, with old songs we applaud nostalgically and new verses to bring us to the present reality, to acknowledge time and their age.

I feed him pieces of the cookies he's given me, to calm him, to divert him from his impatience to be gone to the house that is almost sold, quarters of dark chocolate rounds leaving little brown crumbs in my palm. He takes and eats it each time, while I wonder that we should come to this. What is it that makes us think we are exempt from decay and death so that it always shocks?

Mami has braved the hour-long drive, carsickness, and threatening traffic to see for herself the reality of his most recent decline, to reassure herself he is somewhat content, more or less well taken care of, to be sure she sees him before he dies, to be sure she won't have even more to reproach herself with. To bring back the past a bit, the better bit. But he didn't recognize me a few days ago, talked sentences about work, about home, and doing everything correctly, por lo derecho, in which the words were fine but the whole never went anywhere, never made real sense. I was sad, my face drooping in sympathy with his. I hadn't realized how much I counted on the spark of recognition, the pleased, affectionate look. Now, glowing at Mami, who is insisting he tell us who I am, he claims me too. "Parte de me vida," he says breaking into poetry again instead of the elusive name, "part of my life." The attendant, catching sight of Papi in his revealing shorts, pulls him away from us for a few moments to dress him in a more seemly fashion. He resists but when she coaxes he leaves us for the nearby bathroom. From there his protests erupt, and with them, at last, a name. "°Lola!" he calls out to Mami, his now satisfied, reassured, validated wife, "Lola! Lola!"

1991

What I have lost irretrievably is the expectation of a serene old age rationally planned for. What I have lost is the dream of control. My father planned and arranged everything for his and his wife's old age: house, pension, will, investments, guaranteed everything except his strength of mind. He had been strong-minded, yes. Stubborn. Autocratic. He was always right. You were always wrong. What he liked, everybody had to like. As he said almost to the end, he did everything por lo derecho -- by the right path, morally, correctly. Forget his violence, rages that frightened me to the core when I was young and made my mother even angrier, made her fight him even more. Their relationship was a melodrama, center stage, absorbing all our energy and attention. Just as well. Only dribbles, more than enough, of their angry passion were slapped at our butts and heads.

But his mind gave way. He stopped recognizing the actors on his stage. When my mother couldn't cope with his tattered memory and erratic behavior any longer I put him in a nursing home afraid that he would die there and I would be the murderer. He did die. I am. But only because I believe what he believes: that if you do what's right (por lo derecho) you deserve to have everything come out all right, to have your last years spin out perfectly, spending the money you've saved, living the life you've built.

"Flem!" my mother says of him and tells me it means chock full of chutzpah. And so he was, thinking death and dissolution could be commanded like a dog. Sit! Stay!

What I have gained: a first-hand, front-row, in the round encounter with death and dissolution. Papi lost his memory. He lost his fastidiousness, mercifully, since someone else bathed him, usually against his will, and dressed him in clothes he wouldn't've been seen dead in. He deteriorated between my trips to Puerto Rico but he greeted me with love even if he couldn't find my name, did it till the almost end with that unwearying affection that kept my mother, my sister and me tied to him for decades of fear, anger, and exasperation. It was the last thing to go.

I took pictures of him on his deathbed -- small, small, his thin bones visible beneath the dying skin smoothed over them, shiny and crisp. There were hollows everywhere on his skull. I traced them with my finger as he lay there unmoving, perhaps unseeing, making sounds only when the caretaker turned him from one side to the other to prevent even more bedsores. He lay knees up, fetal, responding positively only to food.

I didn't know he could die like this. I didn't believe, didn't expect this for anyone close to me, for myself. My father who had worked so hard to train me in the fear of men, fire, rape, and deep water didn't recognize this hazard, never warned me about what I could find here, he who warned me about the volatility of money, the perfidy of friends.

Now I know that this can happen to me. I know that the life I've built so carefully is made of dry leaves and a strong wind could blow it away. Papi never taught me that. He has now.

My mother lies in the dark. When you go into the room you can't see to move. My children visit with her in the dark but I feel my way to the windows and open the jalousies a crack. She lies on her back, her head on her brown and gold striped pillowcase with an orange towel between her painful right eye and the blue ice bag. She asks "Quien es?" "Sari," I tell her covered face, "tu hija." She makes her greeting noise, a subdued version of her welcoming shriek, the way she has always greeted any of us when we appeared at her door. I kiss her soft cheek in her still unwrinkled face.

This is the last visit of the trip. I've asked my daughter, son-in-law and granddaughter to stay to visit after me. I don't want to be the last one, the one who leaves her definitely alone, or as alone as you can be in this noisy place. Three times a year I say goodbye and leave her to herself but this time she's on her back. I don't want to go and at the same time I count the minutes to freedom

Is my mother dying? How can I know? When she lies in the dark to ease her eye, which has hurt badly since the stroke, asking the god she hasn't much use for, "Porqué me has dado este dolor?" I'm sure she is. But when she sits up on the edge of the bed and jokes and laughs, I think that all she needs is to sit more, walk more, rehabilitate, as so many have done after more extensive strokes than this.

But she won't sit long. She lies flat asking why she's being punished like this, demanding that any or all of us remove her pain.

"Quítame este dolor. Dame algo para el dolor."

What I want to do is yell at her, "Do something, you passive lump. Of course you hurt. I'd hurt too if I lay in one position twenty-two hours a day."

My mother won't pick up the gauntlet life has thrown at her feet. Instead she rails and curses because it litters her floor.

And she has been crying wolf since I was a child. She has been about to be killed or in such misery she wants to die most of my life. Will I be somewhere else knitting and sipping tea when the wolf comes to devour her?

I've had three bitter fights with Dick since I said, "Adios, Mami. Cuidate. Te quiero mucho." Each time about something gone wrong, like the air conditioner failing in our hotel room after he turned the dial, or the can of olive oil in his suitcase leaking through two plastic bags. Onto what? He hasn't looked, hasn't wiped the suitcase. Each time I feel desperate, violent, as if a tide of olive oil threatens to engulf us while he stands there complacent and unconcerned.

Why? I don't know why. Perhaps because I grew up with violent fights between my parents about small things. Because my mother told me over and over that my father would kill her one day. My sister once found a gun among his clothes. My mother asked me to help her hide it, which I did, putting it in the water of the toilet tank. I am still a young girl trying to make her mother stop giving her the gun to hide.

When she moans, wishing she were dead, asking why she's being punished by life, a line from Carrera Andrade's poem runs through my head. It's what the cicada publishes on a cabbage leaf: "En una hoja de col: / La vida es dura y tuesta el sol." Life, my dear, is hard. The sun is hot. It blisters and burns.

Only death will stop my mother's pain. But I will miss her, the fight in her, her laughter, and yes, (hard to believe I'm saying this) -- her zest for life. I don't want to lose my mother. Ay, Mami! La vida es dura y tuesta el sol.

My mother fell and broke her hip or, perhaps, broke her hip and fell. While I arrange for nurses, worry long distance and book a flight, she is moved from one hospital to another to another in search of any orthopedic surgeon free to operate right then.. After I arrive they drip blood in her veins and blow oxygen into her lungs to strengthen her for the ordeal. Now at last she is in the operating room and my aunt Lydia and I walk the long hall outside her room waiting to know how, or whether, she's survived. She has. They will roll her right out. The surgeon emerges smiling. All, he says, is well.

We walk again, my aunt and I, waiting to see for ourselves. It is then that the head nurse calls to me. She is standing where she can see the young man wheel my mother towards her room. But she's forgotten my name and settles for what she can dredge up. What she shouts down the hall is "Zoraida" And then when I don't respond, "Zoraida! Zoraida!"

It is uncanny. That name is from my childhood, attached to a photograph my mother would pull out with all those other pictures (mostly of people I didn't know) kept in a box beneath her bed. It is the name of the only woman more beautiful than Mami, the only one, other than my lovely mother and of course, Hedy Lamaar, that I ever yearned to look like: long dark hair rippling from my head, brilliant deep dark eyes.

I stride quickly towards the rolling gurney bearing my mother, her hair covered with a cap, a sheet pulled up to her chin. She groans slightly, her eyes closed, a yellow gray tinge to her skin.

Mami breathes now with a tube that sucks the water and phlegm out of her lungs, makes a harsh, continual sound like sucking the last bits of soda from a glass through a straw. She is sleeping now that the painkiller has quieted her and stopped her straining to complain. She can't talk, but with signs or with jagged almost incomprehensible letters laboriously scribed on a piece of paper, she lets us know her wants. That she wants her legs, which have slipped apart, put together again. That she wants me to give her a massage. And when I explain what the technician is doing to her, that he's taking out the liquid in her lungs for her to breathe better, to get better, she mouths, then, in frustration, writes, "Yo no lo creo." She doesn't believe that or any of the other silly, hope-filled things I say. When she goes, whenever that should be, she'll go with the dismissive toss of her head I know so well, with a contemptuous twist of her mouth and eyes. "Tss.Aghgh!"

They have whisked her away and stripped her bed by the time I reach the hospital. She is locked in the morgue and out of reach. I am not allowed to see her. Against the rules, they say. But I want to. They have no right to keep her from me. They have no right to decide for me, no right to protect me from death, from my own mother's death.

I insist on seeing her. Like a manual on assertiveness training, I repeat that I want to say goodbye, that I need to see and touch her for a few minutes. She's my mother and I have a right. I want to see her. Like good bureaucrats, the nurses, the doctor they summon, the head of nursing in her first floor office, all say that it's against the rules. I don't shout or cry or make a fuss, don't even think any more. I simply repeat, "I want to see her." At the sight of anyone at all in a hospital uniform I repeat, "I have a right to see her."

Suddenly they give way. I've won. They will take me to my mother. The head of nursing and a guard with the key accompany Dick and me to the basement room, unlock and slide my mother's gurney out of a low refrigerator. She is wrapped in white plastic taped together with white tape. I'm repelled. She's packaged, like a thing. I have to pull the tape and push back the plastic to touch my mother's refrigerated dead face, gray with death, the tape from the tube to her lungs still about her mouth. I hate this. I shouldn't have come.

I make myself do what I came here to do. I touch and kiss her and wish her goodbye, say, "I'm sorry," and, when I start to cry, feel the nurse's nervous hands pluck me away. Tears must be against the rules too. I leave and walk to the nearest toilet to throw up. But I have nothing in my stomach but my mother, cold and dead and discarded. That, I have to swallow.

"I'm sorry.' I say then, and say again in the days that follow. I'm sorry that you hurt so much, that your last years were so hard. Sorry for your suffering, sorry for your hopes dashed, sorry for your loneliness, for your failures, for your unwillingness, for the love you lacked, for the love you failed to give, for what you wanted and didn't receive, for what you needed to and didn't do. Sorry for whatever failed or failed you. Sorry. I'm so sorry.

My mother lies in state in the funeral home, if "in state" can encompass an ugly looking coffin, an unnatural shaped face unnaturally immobile, and the shoulder pads of her dress pushed up about her ears so that she looks like she has no neck. But from where I sit almost all of Monday and part of Tuesday I can only see her face painted to look natural and alive, ever-present, floating above the rim of the casket in the periphery of my sight. I get used to her presence there. I'm comfortable sitting or standing about the room, with her face as background, talking to relatives whom I've seen throughout this crisis and relatives I've never met or met only at funerals, friends, neighbors, relatives of relatives and the women who tended her at the nursing home. It's a long social affair, a daytime velorio without the food and drink except for an urn of coffee and paper cups in a small basement room.

The incredible chill of the place notwithstanding (and I wear a high necked sweater to withstand it,) I feel a glow of warmth in the meeting and greeting, the sociability of the affair. But Tuesday morning she will be buried. It's final then, this dying business. The dead cannot be kept in the living room forever. The loudspeaker announces the departure for the cemetery. I bury my head on Ade's breast and sob. I sob on Otilia's shoulder, on whoever holds me for a piece. Then they close the coffin lid and her pink face is gone forever.

I walk away from the small crowd under the awning erected at the edge of the burial ground. When the lay preacher my aunts have invited to the funeral stands in front of the casket and begins his long-winded sermonizing, I just take off between the rows of flat stones each with one or two small plaques inscribed with a name, a date of birth, a date of death, each with two metal vases filled with artificial flowers. When I look up I am in a large flat field dotted with plastic pink and yellow and blue laid out in double rows. I was shown Papi's grave the day before in the patch called Los Jazmines -- not a jasmine in sight -- at a location titled DD34. Where the stone had been is a deep hole with a cement box at the bottom and a heap of red earth beside it. Between two other graves lies Papi's (and soon Mami's) stone. I sit on it and look at the plasticky view, at the crumbling red clay, at the reinitas darting and dashing across the empty air to a lone clump of trees, at the larger darker birds squawking further away. Anywhere but behind me where that man is going on and on and my mother lies in a closed coffin on a small table.

Something warns me in time to turn and see six men, Dick among them, strain at the handles of the heavy coffin, lift it off the table under the awning, and carry it toward me. I watch as they position it on the straps across the hole, watch the machinery lower it, watch the workmen pull the straps out from under it and roll them up. I take a clod of that familiar red earth and throw it on the coffin and start back, past where my aunts and uncles still sit and stand, to a large palm tree. I hide behind it, lean my head on the rough surface of the trunk and weep.

Dulce de Naranja

In Puerto Rico, Las Navidades is a season, not a single day. Early in December, with the hurricane season safely over, the thick autumn rains withdraw and sun pours down on the island uninterrupted. This will be a problem by March, when the reservoirs empty, and the shores of Lake Luchetti show wider and wider rings of red mud, until the lake bottom curls up into little pancakes of baked clay and the skeletons of long drowned houses are revealed. Then, people wait anxiously for rain, and pray that the sweet, white coffee blossoms of April don't wither on the branch. But during Navidades, the sun shines on branches heavily laden with hard green berries starting to ripen and turn red. Oranges glow on the trees, aguinaldos dominate the airwaves of Radio Café and women start grating yuca and plantain for pasteles, and feeling up the pigs and chickens, calculating the best moment for the slaughter.

It was 1962 or maybe 1965. Any one of those years. Barrio Indiera Baja of Maricao and Barrio Rubias of Yauco are among the most remote inhabited places on the island, straddling the crest of the Cordillera Central among the mildewed ruins of old coffee plantations, houses and sheds left empty when the tides of international commerce withdrew. A century ago, Yauco and Maricao fought bitterly to annex this highland acreage from one another, at a time when Puerto Rican coffee was the best in the world. But Brazil flooded the market with cheaper, faster growing varieties. There were hurricanes and invasions and the coffee region slid into decline.

In the 1960s of my childhood most people in Indiera still worked in coffee, but everyone was on food stamps except the handful of hacendados, and young people kept leaving for town jobs or for New York and Connecticut.

Those were the years of modernization. Something was always being built or inaugurated—dams, bridges, new roads, shopping centers and acres of housing developments. Helicopters crossed the mountains installing electrical poles in places too inaccessible for trucks (keeping an eye out for illegal rum stills.) During my entire childhood the aqueducto, the promise of running water, inched its way towards us with much fanfare and very little result. When the pipes were finally in place, the engineers discovered that there was rarely enough pressure to drive the water up the steep slopes north of the reservoir. About once a month the faucets, left open all the time, started to sputter. Someone called out "aqueduuuuucto" and everyone ran to fill their buckets before the pipes went dry again.

Navidades was the season for extravagance in the midst of hardship. Food was saved up and then lavishly spread on the table. New clothing was bought in town or made up by a neighbor and furniture brought home, to be paid off in installments once the harvest was in.

One of those years, her husband bought Doña Gina an indoor stove with an oven, and all the neighbors turned out to see. They were going to roast the pig indoors! Not a whole pig, of course, but I was there watching when Don Lencho slashed the shaved skin and rubbed the wounds with handfuls of mashed garlic and fresh oregano, achiote oil and vinegar, black pepper and salt. Doña Gina was making arroz con dulce, tray after tray of cinnamon-scented rice pudding with coconut. The smells kept all the children circling around the kitchen like hungry sharks.

This was before every house big enough for a chair had sprouted a TV antenna. My brother and I went down to the Canabal house to watch occasional episodes of Bonanza dubbed into Spanish: I liked to watch the lips move out of sync with the voice that said "Vámonos, Hoss!" And by 1966 there would be a TV in the seventh grade classroom at Arturo Lluberas Junior High, down near Yauco, where the older girls would crowd in to watch "El Show del Mediodía." But in Indiera and Rubias nobody was hooked on TV Christmas specials yet. When the season began, people still tuned up their cuatros and guitars, took down the güiros and maracas and started going house-to-house looking for free drinks. So while Don Lencho kept opening the oven to baste the pig, Chago and Nestor and Papo played aguinaldos and plenas and Carmencita improvised lyrics back and forth with Papo, each trying to top the other in witty commentary, the guests hooting and clapping when one or the other scored a hit. No one talked much about Cheito and Luis away in Viet Nam, or Adita's fiancé running off with a pregnant high school girl a week before the wedding or Don Toño coughing up blood all the time. "Gracias a Dios" said Doña Gina, "Aqui estamos."

During Navidades the cars of city relatives started showing up parked in the road next to the red and green jeeps. My girlfriends had to stay close to home and wear starched dresses, and the boys looked unnaturally solemn in ironed white shirts, with their hair slicked down. Our relatives were mostly in New York, but sometimes a visitor came all that way, announced ahead of time by letter, or, now and then, adventurous enough to try finding our farm with just a smattering of Spanish and a piece of paper with our names.

The neighbors grew their own gandules and plantain, but except for a few vegetables we didn't farm our land. My father drove to San Juan every week to teach at the university, and did most of our shopping at the Pueblo supermarket on the way out of town. Sometimes all those overflowing bags of groceries weighed on my conscience, especially when I went to the store with my best friend Tita and waited while she asked Don Paco to put another meager pound of rice on their tab. My father was a biologist and a commuter. This was how we got our frozen blintzes and English muffins, fancy cookies and date nut bread.

But during Navidades it seemed, for a little while, as if everyone had enough. My father brought home Spanish turrón-—sticky white nougat full of almonds, wrapped in thin edible layers of papery white stuff. The best kind is the hard turrón you have to break with a hammer. Then there were all the gooey, intensely sweet fruit pastes you eat with crumbly white cheese. The dense, dark red-brown of guayaba, golden mango, sugar-crusted pale brown batata and dazzlingly white coconut. And my favorite, dulce de naranja, a tantalizing mix of bitter orange and sugar, the alternating tastes always startling on the tongue. We didn't eat pork, but my father cooked canned corned beef with raisins and onions and was the best Jewish tostón maker in the world.

Christmas trees were still a strange gringo custom for most of our neighbors, but each year we picked something to decorate, this household of transplanted New Yorkers—my Puerto Rican mother, my Jewish father and the two, then three of us "Americanito" kids growing up like wild guayabas on an overgrown and half-abandoned coffee farm. One year we cut a miniature grove of bamboo and folded dozens of tiny origami cranes in gold and silver paper to hang on the branches. Another year it was the tightly rolled, flame red flowers of señorita with traditional, shiny Christmas balls glowing among the lush green foliage. Sometimes it was boughs of Australian pine hung with old ornaments we brought with us from New York in 1960, those pearly ones with the inverted cones carved into their sides like funnels of fluted silver and gold light.

The only telephone was the one at the crossroads, which rarely worked, so other than my father's weekly trip to San Juan, the mail was our only link with the world outside the barrio. Every day during las Navidades when my brother and I stopped at the crossroads for the mail there would be square envelopes in bright colors bringing Season's Greetings from far away people we'd never met. But there were also packages. We had one serious sweet tooth on each side of the family. Every year my Jewish grandmother sent metal tins full of brightly wrapped toffee in iridescent paper that my brother and I saved for weeks. Every year my Puerto Rican grandfather sent boxes of Jordan almonds in sugary pastels and jumbo packs of Hershey's kisses and Tootsie rolls.

Of course, this was also the season of rum, of careening jeep loads of festive people in constant motion up and down the narrow twisting roads of the mountains. You could hear the laughter and loud voices fade and blare as they wound in and out of the curves. All along the roadsides were shrines, white crosses or painted rocks with artificial flowers and the dates of horrible accidents: head-on collisions when two jeeps held onto the crown of the road too long; places where drivers mistook the direction of the next dark curve and rammed into a tree, or plummeted, arcing into the air and over the dizzying edge, to crash down among the broken branches of citrus and poma-rosa leaving a wake of destruction. Some of those ravines still held the rusted frames of old trucks and cars no one knew how to retrieve after the bodies were taken home for burial.

It was rum, the year my best friend's father died. Early Navidades, just coming into December and parties already in full swing. Chiqui, Tita, Chinita and I spent a lot of time out in the road, while inside, women in black dresses prayed, cleaned and cooked. Every so often one of them would come out on the porch and call Tita or Chiqui, who were cousins, to get something from the store, or go down the hill to the spring to fetch another couple of buckets of water.

No one in Indiera was called by their real name. It was only in school, when the teacher took attendance, that you found out all those Tatas and Titas, Papos and Juniors were named Milagros and Carmen María, Jose Luis and Dionisio. The few names people used became soft and blurred in our mouths, in the country Puerto Rican Spanish we inherited from Andalucian immigrants who settled in those hills centuries ago and kept as far as they could from Church and State alike. We mixed yanqui slang with the archaic accents of the sixteenth century so that Ricardo became Hicaldo while Wilson turned into Güilsong. Every morning the radio announced all the saints whose names could be given to children born that day, which is presumably how people ended up with names like Migdonio, Eduvigis and Idelfonso.

Anyway, Tita's father was dying of alcoholism, his liver finally surrendering to forty or fifty years of heavy drinking and perhaps his heart collapsing under the weight of all the beatings and abuse he had dished out to his wife and fourteen children. Tita was his youngest child—ten, scrawny, fast on her feet. Her city nieces and nephews were older, but in the solemn days of waiting for death, she played her status for all it was worth, scolding them for laughing or playing, reminding them that she was their aunt, and must be respected. All day the women swept and washed and cooked and in the heat of the afternoon sat sipping coffee, talking softly on the porch.

In our classroom, where we also awaited news of the death, we were deep into the usual holiday rituals of public school. The girls cut out poinsettia flowers from red construction paper and the boys got to climb on chairs to help Meesee Torres hang garishly colored pictures of the Three Kings above the blackboard. We practiced singing "Alegria, Alegria, Alegria" and during Spanish class we read stories of miraculous generosity and goodwill.

Late one Tuesday afternoon after school, we heard the wailing break out across the road and the next day Meesee Torres made us all line up and walk up the hill to Tita's house to pay our respects. We filed into their living room, past the open coffin, each placed a single flower in the vase Meessee had brought, then filed out again. What astonished me was how small Don Miguel looked, nested in white satin, just a little brown man without those bulging veins of rage at his temples and the heavy hands waiting to hit.

The next night the velorio began. The road was full of jeeps and city cars, and more dressed up relatives than ever before spilled out of the little house. For three days people ate and drank and prayed and partied, laughing and chatting, catching up on old gossip and rekindling ancient family arguments. Now and then someone would have to separate a couple of drunken men preparing to hit out with fists. Several of the women had ataques, falling to the ground and tearing their hair and clothing.

The first night of the velorio was also the first night of Hanukkah that year. While Tita went to church with her mother to take part in rosarios and novenas and Catholic mysteries I knew nothing of, my family sat in the darkened living room of our house lighting the first candle on the menorah, the one that lights all the others. Gathered around that small glow, my father told the story of the Macabees who fought off an invading empire, while across the road, Tita's family laughed together, making life bigger than death. I remember sitting around the candles, thinking of those ancient Jews hanging in for thirty years to take back their temple, what it took to not give up; and of all the women in the barrio raising children who sometimes died and you never knew who would make it and who wouldn't, of people setting off for home and maybe meeting death in another jeep along the way. And in the middle of a bad year, a year of too much loss, there were still two big pots of pasteles and a house full of music and friends. Life, like the aqueducto, seemed to be unpredictable, maddening and sometimes startlingly abundant.

That night I lay awake for a long time in the dark, listening to life walking towards me. Luis would never come home from Viet Nam and Cheito would come home crazy, but the war would end someday and most of us would grow up. My father would be fired from the university for protesting that war, and we would be propelled into a new life, but I would find lifelong friends and new visions for myself in that undreamt of city. Death and celebration, darkness and light, the miraculous star of the Three Kings and the miracle of a lamp burning for eight days on just a drop of oil. So much uncertainty and danger and so much stubborn faith. And somewhere out there in the dark, beyond the voices of Tita's family, still murmuring across the road, the three wise mysterious travelers were already making their way to me, carrying something unknown, precious, strange.

chicken house goat girls

We were the only girls who wore pants, she said, sitting across the orange plastic table at a fast food joint in Brooklyn, forty years after we said goodbye on a rainy morning in late spring in the cordillera of our hearts. Now we live in cities but we both dream in unfurling fern leaves under the shade of towering pomarosas. We still have red clay mud in our bellies, in our pores, in every cell. What we are made of: mud, pomarosa, cold spring water.

Among all the skirted girls of the barrio, among all the women in their flowered cotton dresses worn thin from pounding on river rocks, among all the women and girls sitting on porches shelling beans at dusk, I answer, we were the only ones who climbed trees, *guamá, guayaba, flamboyán, pino*, the only girls with skinned knees and burrs in our hair, with dirt under our nails, the only girls who let the dogs sniff our crotches and laughed. *No seas cabra*, the neighbor women would snap, and their daughters would settle back onto the porches and smooth their skirts down, waiting to be called on. You and I, we bucked and skipped and played with boys, and ran shouting through the dusk among the fireflies.

La vieja told me her Taino grandmother was caught stealing food on the hacienda, decked only in her long black hair, was hunted with dogs, locked in a room, forced into a dress and a marriage. The rest of her life they called her La Tormenta because she would as soon smack a man across the face with a dried salt cod as look at him. But she taught her granddaughter how to make the birthing mats, where to dig for the best roots, how to keep her own name in a secret place under her tongue, at the back of her knees, a dark pool of knowing.

We would steal fruit from fenced-in trees, run from dogs, take off our clothes, throw rocks at our enemies. We had our own rebellions.

Do you remember the chicken house? she asks and I think *the smell of fertilizer*, sacks of it piled in the back, old broken furniture, hoes and rakes, an outgrown tricycle. Of course I do. Her skinny little hips, lying back on a bag of clothes, the cement floor, sunbeams full of dust motes, the hummingbirds in the bushes, the lizards skittering up the walls, thickets of ginger standing guard, and two girls with Taino eyes, our hair full of twigs, dirt under our nails, laughing as we sniffed, our scabbed knees parted, digging for roots.

Cosecha

She leaned up on the travel agent's too high counter and signed the check—Esther Rabinowitz Hernandez—with her mind on what she must not under any conditions leave out of the suitcase she was hastily packing. She usually traveled with plenty of lead time to make lists and even lists of lists, but she'd only gotten the telegram that afternoon and she had to be on the plane tomorrow morning. With her daughter Rebecca, knock on wood, who should by now be on the highway from Boston. She looked at her watch. Somewhere around New Haven if she'd left when she said she would. Which was not likely. Rebecca took after her grandmothers, both of them, who never got anywhere less than thirty minutes late. Since her own exasperating mother was one of those two ladies, her daughter's lackadaisical sense of time left her restless with annoyance.

Pepa was sick. At least that's what the telegram had said. But Pepa was 86 years old and Maria, Esther's mother-in-law and Pepa's daughter, was as mealy mouthed as she was disorganized, so the old woman was probably dying, if not dead, right this minute. She looked at her watch again. She wanted to hurry the travel agent, to rush through the streets to her apartment, to throw things in the suitcase with abandon, to speed through the streets to the airport, to be in the remote hamlet in western Puerto Rico in an impossibly short time, to see Pepa once more before she died. She was angry at Rebecca for making her wait for tomorrow morning's flight even though tonight's flight was full, even though one of the reasons Rebecca had dropped everything to drive down and fly with her tomorrow was that Esther didn't want to do the trip alone. She forced herself to take time thanking the travel agent, putting the tickets away, walking the ten blocks to her home.

The next morning she woke Rebecca at six, pressed her lips tight at Rebecca's protesting moans, shook her head at Rebecca's long luxurious shower. She only nibbled at her bagel, sipped at her coffee and, when her daughter finally appeared, greeted her by asking, "Is that what you're wearing?," with a gesture at Rebecca's worn blue jeans. "What's wrong with what I'm wearing?" Rebecca started to answer automatically and was shocked at feeling the familiar stubborn adolescent resistance take over her body. She stopped herself at the "What ... ?" pretending she hadn't quite heard. Esther muttered "never mind" and stomped off to her bedroom to check her suitcase again. Rebecca thought of the long hours the two of them would be cooped up together not just in the taxi and the plane but on the long drive from San Juan through Ponce to Yauco to Indiera. And if someone didn't arrange to have a jeep at the road's edge they would have a twenty minute walk up the muddy rutted trail to Pepa's cabin at the end of all that hard traveling. The green skirt, maybe. And the gold print rayon blouse.

Her mother slept most of the flight. Rebecca tried to read but her mind kept rearranging the details of the car rental and rehearsing the route through the edges of the city over the mountains past Caguas and Cayey. This worked very nicely to keep her from exploring the deep certainty she felt that she would never see her beloved 'buela Pepa again. It was three months since that first mild heart attack but according to the family she'd been complaining about one thing or another, headaches and insomnia and diarrhea since then. And they said her mind was going. That was hard to believe but Anselma, who took care of her and was her best friend, was so upset by how secretive and angry she'd become that even Esther had reluctantly accepted her verdict. Both Esther and Rebecca had been mourning for months, mourning Pepa's bright eyes, her strength, her honesty, her affection for la americana: the grand daughter-in-law that she preferred infinitely to her own sappy youngest daughter, Rebecca's grandmother Maria. "¡Que mujer mas changa!" was all she had to say about her. And Bequita la americanita, how she loved her Bequita. It was no use. Rebecca cried her way over the Atlantic while her mother gently snored.

Esther was right. Her mother-in-law had worded the telegram and Pepa was not just sick, she was dying and she knew it. She had refused food for two days now and could barely swallow the water Anselma gently dripped into her mouth. She lay in her own high bed in the small bedroom facing the western slopes of the farm, of the island. On a clear day she could see Desecheo through the window, a little hump of an island on the horizon. Today was a hazy day and Pepa's eyes were closed, but not because she was sleeping. Sometimes she had a hard time knowing if she was dreaming or remembering or awake. Like now: was that Maria in the room with her complaining, or was it before, when Pepa was young and could lift a fifty pound sack of rice with one arm? ¡Esa Maria! Desde niña una sapa. Queja tras queja. She still whined. Lord, get her away from me or I'll let myself die so I won't have to hear her again. Maria's husband had left her ages ago, the only smart thing that sinvergüenza ever did.

The money! She had to stay awake to find the money. She had to give it to the girls before she died. She saw them then, the tight green rolls of bills spinning away from her faster than she could crawl after them. She moaned and felt the pillow shift beneath her head, the drops of water fall on her lips.

Tired and sad though they were, and angry at themselves for not visiting Pepa while she was still relatively well, Esther and Rebecca nevertheless felt a surge of happiness when the cool breeze at el dieciocho blew in from the uninterrupted expanse beyond Rebecca's left shoulder. This spot was the unmarked boundary between plain and mountain, a piece of road approximately eighteen kilometers up from Yauco that looked down on the lean steep hills plunging sharply back toward town. They were almost there. Esther looked at Rebecca's smiling profile and thought of Rafael and how proud he would have been of his daughter if he'd been alive and here to watch her drive competently along the roads of his childhood. They passed the school he went to when he lived with his grandmother, until he was thirteen. That was when his parents had taken him to New York and Junior high school number 98 or 99 or some such thing.

Rebecca nodded. "I was thinking of Papi," she said as she swerved nimbly to avoid a truck racing down the middle of the road around a sharp steep turn.

"Of course," her mother answered.

After all it was his overpowering nostalgia for the place of his childhood that had brought them here over twenty five years ago, in the face of Esther's passive resistance. Becca was just three when they first climbed this road to a remote farm, three thousand feet from sea level and a mile from the nearest paved road. Nothing in Esther's Brooklyn childhood had prepared her for the exuberance of the vegetation or of his family's welcome.

Anselma moved slowly, not just because she was feeling every one of her more than seventy years. Not only because she did not want to disturb her aunt who was snoring lightly and lying so unnaturally still beneath the white candlewick bedspread, but because it was her nature to move deliberately. Beneath her breath she murmured "Ave Maria, madre de Diós, sanctificada..." the rhythm of the prayer, of the rosary, as familiar as her heartbeat. From here she could hear the burble of their voices, of Maria, Tita, and Manuel out on the porch. Quick exchanges, fast paced inquiry and response. Even Maria's complaints—she had an unimaginably painful migraine, she said—even that sounded like the swift scurrying feet of rats on the plafón of Pepa's house at night.

She missed Pepa so much. She'd had to cook the meals by herself for weeks without Pepa's strong hands, her familiar presence. Even young Tita, who usually hung about the kitchen and peeled the guineos, was out talking to Manuel, who hadn't visited his mother in over a year. If Pepa had been up and about she would have had something to say to him about that, and she would have told Maria to get her own water when she wanted to swallow another of those pastillas of hers during the meal, instead of asking her overworked cousin to fetch it.

She was tired. She'd had all the nursing to do—with some help from Tina and Doña Fela of course—but she hadn't slept a whole night in two weeks. And then there was the sadness. Pepa had changed, once she knew she was dying, and Anselma believed her aunt had known that for months. It hurt so much to have Pepa treat her with such mistrust, to hide what she was doing when her niece came into the room. Tears came into her eyes as she remembered, as she re-cited softly. "Padre nuestro que estás en los cielos..." as she bundled up the wet sheets, the soiled nightgown, the wrinkled pillowcase. Someone else would have to wash them. She felt too old.

Maria's head hurt. It had been hurting without respite since she'd stepped across the threshold of her childhood home two days ago. She had always hated living in this dreary cabin, with cracks between its plain board walls, with holes in the floor you could see through. The others had played games, throwing things on the chickens down below but she'd been very little, frightened that something would reach up and snatch at her. It wasn't anything she would admit to anyone, but she'd hated her childhood. The others, her sisters and brothers and cousins, always laughed at her. They called her boba and sapa. And her mother smacked her for crying to be carried over the hole in the door sill. Although she tried never to let it show, she'd always hated her mother too. She still hated her, God help her. But now that that mujer maldita was at last going to die, now that she was going to be free of her, she was frightened. And sad. Horribly sad. She couldn't understand it. She could only feel it taking over her head, filling it with a dull, overpowering pain that brought tears to her eyes and made her sick to her stomach. She heard herself whisper "No te mueras. No te mueras. Please don't die," and turned pale. Then she threw up over the roots of the sour orange tree.

Manuel waited patiently, arms crossed on his chest, leaning on the jeep that was going to take him to his car which would take him to Ponce to the Hotel Intercontinental where he'd booked a room for the night. It was a two hour ride but nothing on earth would induce him to accept any of the lumpy, maybe buggy mattresses, covered with clean, worn, but sometimes stained sheets, that he would be offered at any relative's or neighbor's house. He'd done enough of that when he was younger. Last time he'd stayed next door at Doña Fela's, trying to read his newspaper, when it finally got to him at least a day late, by the light of a dim bare bulb high in the ceiling. No thank you! It was a very long time indeed since he'd had to live like that.

He was fond of his mother, came whenever he was sent for, sent her money regularly and expensive gifts on her birthday, saint's day and Christmas and would genuinely miss the old lady when she died. But how she could still live in this hole, buried alive up here…No, *back* here. Backward. This barrio was twenty-five years behind the times. And his mother was fifty years behind the barrio.

He looked at the house in front of him. It didn't deserve the term house. A shed, falling apart, the wooden boards rotting, the zinc roof red with rust. How it had stood through the last hurricane he didn't know. And those shutters that made the rooms dark as the tomb when they were closed to keep the rain out. He shook his head in puzzlement and disbelief. He had long since stopped trying to make her move in with him. He'd given up offering to build her a good cement house or to install plumbing or a telephone. Oh! He just didn't understand. He shook his head slowly, lips pursed. He didn't understand her at all.

Inside the house Pepa lay still, thinking of the money. She wanted it for school, for Mercedita to go to nursing school, for Moncho to buy books. She herself had never gone beyond ninth grade. Her brother José Manuel had. A long time ago. He'd gone to Rio Piedras to study and for a while he'd worked as a rural teacher, before he gave it up to become a builder. She begged but her family wouldn't send her. When she married Luisito she'd gone to the high in town for a semester before she became pregnant. And then they moved up here. All her grandchildren had finished high school. She started naming them—Consuelo, Rafael, Benjamin—but gave it up to think of her great-grandchildren. Several had at least started at the university and two had finished. She was sure of at least two. It was hard to count now.

La americanita, Rafael's child, she went to a school for art after high school. She hadn't needed Pepa's help then, but now Rafael was dead and the child needed to stop working at that printing place for a while and paint and paint. Pepa looked at the picture that Becca had made for her of the house and the garden and the view to the west. It was painted at sunrise, her favorite time, and you could see that in the painting, the light kind and soft, pearly with a tiny bit of pink in the sky so faint you hardly noticed it if you didn't look for it. She studied the painting as if it were in front of her but the picture was behind her, her eyes were closed, and she lay unmoving upon the bed.

Esther and Rebecca were exhausted by the time they bounced up the rutted red clay road past Anselma's pink cement house. Past Doña Fela's garden. And past the small grey cement box of a house Pepa had abandoned after her husband died in its back bedroom. That was when she'd moved back into the cabin on the ridge that had been their first home in Indiera and which, miraculously, still held together. As her mother hugged the weeping Anselma, Rebecca looked in the door at the wide hand sawn floorboards with the arcs of the saw still on them seventy years later. Those boards, this house, the cool breeze blowing from one end of it to the other, the faint smell of Maja soap on Anselma's body as she hugged her, all of them were as familiar as her face in the mirror in the

morning.

She stood by the door of the room while her mother went up to Doña Pepa's bed, kissed her cheek and whispered her name. She wasn't sad now, only at peace, at home. Over the old woman's head the painting Rebecca had done ten years ago was caught in a stray ray of the setting sun and shone like the dawn. Rebecca turned and walked quietly to the kitchen for a glass of water. She would go and sit with her great-grandmother, her very grand great-grandmother, when Esther and Anselma had left.

Pepa's eyes moved behind her lids scanning scenes from her life and now many more of them were about money. About wanting money to have a tooth put in where Luis had knocked one out the time when he'd drunk himself angry after the hurricane. About Don Alejandro at the store adding up their debts in the school notebook he kept under the counter, a long list of figures representing rice and beans and tomato sauce and bacalao and Luis's rum. A line and under it a sum that would eat up their coffee harvest.

About hiding money in the empty cigarette package behind the picture of Christ on the cross where she kept the rolled up dollar bills she earned by selling eggs or sewing a school uniform for Doña Magda's daughter.

About the money Manuel began sending as soon as he'd paid off his school debts, most of it still nestled in the space between the old wall and the new one behind the bed she lay in. It was usually so comforting to know it was there. But now she was restless when she thought of it.

She'd reached in there for a couple of hundred for Juancito for the jeep he needed to market his produce and quietly, quietly, a few more hundreds for Elena to get an abortion. No one need ever know. And the girl could accept that job in the mayor's office in Mayagüez.

She'd spoken to her granddaughter , la licenciada, years ago, to make sure the cash went to the girls, to do it up all very legal. She was angry when she found out she couldn't leave her house and money where she wanted. By law two thirds of everything went to her sons and daughter who didn't need it, except maybe Maria. But the other third would definitely go to Rebecca and Mercedita. And more, much more, if she could manage it without someone finding out.

But the money wasn't behind her bed any more and sometimes she

remembered where she had put it and sometimes she didn't. If she showed Bequita or Mercedita where it was, they could take it out without the family or the lawyers knowing. She had hidden it for them. She opened her eyes briefly and saw that Becca was there. She would talk to her about it when she wasn't so tired.

Esther couldn't get to sleep. She lay in Anselma's spare bedroom in a big mahogany bed and twitched and turned and rearranged herself for an hour before sitting up and turning on the room light. She was anxious, restless, and nervy. She hadn't smoked in ten years but she was dying for a cigarette.

The floor tiles felt cold to her bare feet and little drafts of chill night air brought goose bumps to her arms and legs. She put her cotton sweater over her shoulders before she felt her way down the hall to the little room Rebecca had claimed for her own. It was the old maid's room, from when the house belonged to the Masetti family and now held a narrow iron bed and a large refrigerator which was used to house the overflow from Anselma's grandson's colmado. And to keep Pepa's perishables: the milk for her coffee, the meat in small packages to match her appetite.

Esther scratched at the door, hoping Rebecca was awake and not wanting to wake her if she was asleep, even though she was prepared to be annoyed if she was. But Becca was awake, journal held open in her hand, the page full of words and drawings, drawings and words, what else?

Rebecca scuttled backwards on the bed to let Esther climb on. But not before leaning out to open the fridge door for a small can of pear nectar for her mother. She sat back against the hard cold bedstead, sipping guava juice and listening to her mother's familiar complaints about how hard it was to sleep in alien beds. She was glad her mother had come. She'd been writing about how out of place she'd felt at dinner, how sensitive to her differentness. Especially with the women. It was as if they had a secret she would never know. Or that whatever she did was always just a little bit wrong. It wasn't true with 'buela Pepa, only with the others. She'd never figured it out.

She'd been drawing more than writing because she couldn't write about what she couldn't understand and so there were sketches of Anselma's feet in low-heeled pink slippers, of the view out of Pepa's room where she sat for hours while Anselma's slippers caressed the worn wood floor going from the bed to the bureau to the bed to the door. While several neighbors, people she didn't recognize but who recognized her, looked in, prayed quietly, and left. While Pepa slept, stirred and moaned, and slept again.

Watching her mother bite at her cuticles, something she hadn't done in months, Rebecca felt a huge wave of sadness envelope her. She interrupted Esther to tell her "You miss Papi," and Esther's face crumpled. She waved her juice wildly about until Rebecca took it from her and put it on the floor. Then Esther laid her head down on her knees and sobbed. It was five years since Rafael's sudden death but it still surprised them, the freshness of the sorrow and the suddenness and unexpectedness of its attack. But they should have anticipated it this time. Rebecca sat beside her mother patting her hair smooth and letting her own tears run down her cheeks and fall silently on her lap.

Anselma was in the kitchen heating milk for her coffee by the light of the full moon that spilled in through the open window, when her aunt stopped breathing. She took her steaming cup into the bedroom and set it on the bureau to cool for a little while. How Pepa loved her coffee. She felt guilty not sharing this cup with her. She picked up the washcloth to clean the spittle leaking out of Pepa's mouth and started to wipe it before she noticed the stillness, stiller than before. She leaned in to catch the wisp of breath from Pepa's nose but felt nothing. She finished wiping the mouth, the chin, then walked slowly over to the bureau for the clothes she'd put aside to change Pepa into when she died. But when she reached the bed she felt so weak she had to sit down abruptly on the chair she'd spent so much time on in the last weeks. She felt desolately lonely.

She had been closer to Pepa in the last ten years than she had ever been to her two husbands or her children. They had both been old and widowed when they began their real friendship, so different from what it had been before. And no one, she was sure, could understand what Pepa meant to her. She couldn't herself. This was not an aunt she was going to bury. This was her protector, her companion. If people didn't have such dirty minds she would say Pepa was like a husband to her even if they lived in two houses. They had cooked together, gardened together, sewed together, listened to the novelas together, talked together, planned everything together. She was sharp tongued, that Pepa of hers, but never with her. And they told each other everything, which was why it hurt so much it made her breath catch that Pepa had tried to keep a secret from her.

But Anselma knew more than Pepa, in her craziness at the end, had imagined. Anselma knew that most of the money was gone from behind the bed and that Pepa was trying to get around the law by hiding it somewhere else. Papa Dios only knew where. Not far. The poor woman couldn't move far even before she was bedridden. She'd taken it hard, her helplessness. "Ay Pepa," she sighed. "How will I live without you?" She lowered her knees carefully to the rough wooden floor, leaned her head against Pepa's cooling hand and began again to recite: "Ave Maria, llena de gracia ..."

Rebecca went to the latrine to cry. The small outhouse was ancient, the wood silvery with age. When, after years of use, the latrine got filled, another hole was dug, the small structure was lifted and dragged over to it, then the old hole was topped off with dirt and a tree planted. Through the cracks in the door Rebecca could see the shaded path through all those trees to the kitchen window. The house was filling with strangers who were spilling out into the yard. She had come here to escape them. She sat on the edge of the seat one hand caressing the wood made smooth by years of bare bottoms, the other holding toilet paper that she wiped across her eyes every few minutes in a vain attempt to stem the tears. It was appalling how much she hurt right down her middle, so that she sat bent over to keep it from spilling out over her feet.

She was crying not only for Pepa but also for her own lost childhood, for her father, for illusions of safety. It had hit her, looking at Pepa's unmoving face, at Anselma's worn one, that her mother was going to die. Maybe soon. Maybe, like her father, suddenly. One minute he was laughing, the way he did everything, big and loud, and the next he was lying on the rug, grey and dying. He had not made it to the hospital. And Rebecca who had lived the five years before that moment savoring her independence from her parents, became a lost child again. That was what she was now. A child. Lost, hiding out in the bathroom from the hurtful adults who ruled her life. She sat there, alone, her face contorted with crying, little wads of wet toilet paper at her feet, sobbing quietly, steadily, while her mother, sad and lonely herself, looked for her everywhere.

It wasn't until the funeraria had come and taken Pepa away that Anselma gave in to the feelings behind her eyes and in her stomach that had been slowing her down all morning. The porch and the tiny sala were full of neighbors and friends, the noise of their talk drumming insistently on her like heavy drops hitting the metal roof in rainy season. The sounds were loud, constant, inescapable, at least until she fainted and left them behind. She woke to find herself in Pepa's spare bedroom, in the bed she'd stolen some sleep in during the weeks past. It was quiet now. Someone must have swept the people away. Someone had. Her neighbor, Fela, had asked them all over to her porch and sala, at least until Anselma recovered from the first shock of her loss, and her sons and daughter and other family started arriving. Until she got up to serve rum and anisette and coffee with the help of her American daughter-in-law, and with Fela's own help of course. She had sent her grandson to Doña Sarita, who had roasted a fresh batch of coffee beans yesterday, and to the store for the bread to serve with it.

It was a velorio even without the body, which was having unnecessary things done to it at the funeraria. Anselma remembered the velorio after her mother had died of bladder cancer. Mamita had lain in her bedroom while in the living room her family and friends had sat all night, talking, drinking, praying, eating. One after another they had all stepped in to see the woman they had known all their lives, sick and well, young and old, and now dead. These days you were sent to the funeral parlor to see the dead, to sit in their pew-like benches, gossiping in front of the ornate coffin. But this was Pepa who had died. Pepa who would come back and haunt their pastel painted cement houses if they did it that way, and funeraria or no funeraria, friends began to gather at the neighbor's house and then after dark at Pepa's.

Maria took over in the kitchen. Anselma would have been surprised, if she had been up and about, and conscious of anything but the growing thickness in her chest, and the heat of her fever. Maria strained the coffee, rinsed the colander, and strained another batch, over and over. She washed the cups and glasses as Tina and Becca and Manuel's overdressed granddaughter brought them in from Pepa's living room, kitchen, porch, and yard. Mercedita appeared briefly in the doorway. Also la licenciada. But they left Maria, grim-faced and probably headachy, to her work. But, no. Her head didn't hurt. She was not feeling anything, her mind fully on the black coffee streaming out of the point of the cloth filter as she raised it above the pot.

Inside the house, Manuel and his eldest sat very formally on the wicker sofa. As people came in they shook hands and exchanged a few words with them, then retreated to the porch, where it was livelier. Of Pepa and Luisito's children, only three were still alive. The third, José, was sick in Cincinnati and sent a telegram. Six of the grandchildren were in distant places on the globe, with one in Germany and another in Hawaii. But that one, Richard, the one in Honolulu, had never known his grandmother. Unlike Rafael he'd been born and raised in New Jersey knowing no Spanish. His parents never took him to the island, and when he visited once on vacation he didn't call on any relatives. He didn't know them or care about them.

Of the great-grandchildren there were three that were good friends with Pepa. One of them, Leila, was on the porch sipping rum. And scattered about the house and yard were some of the children Pepa had helped raise long after hers had grown up, and *their* children and grandchildren, three of them babies. There were neighbors, ex-neighbors, friends of her grandchildren, schoolmates of her great-grandchildren, friends of friends, a few, who'd heard about her and without knowing exactly where she lived, without having met her, had once or twice traveled all the way back into the mountains to the farm. Gary, who now lived in Hato Rey had known no Spanish and communicated in hand signals and with the translation services of a neighbor child whose English was still of the *girl, boy, dog* variety which had added to the hilarity of the visit. He heard about Pepa's death from Leila's boyfriend, left work in mid-afternoon, rented a car and drove into the mountains to say good-bye. Her body was long gone by the time he arrived but she was still here, he was sure of it, serving coffee, giving Anselma one of her sidelong glances, twisting her mouth impatiently at Maria or Manuel or the neighbor's boy who kept dangling from the porch rail until his father picked him up and pushed him across the road to bed.

Maria and Rebecca didn't go to the funeral, partly to take care of Anselma who needed to be in the hospital but refused to go. They fed her the antibiotics her doctor grandson had prescribed and the herbs she demanded in a hoarse whisper. But Maria also cherished the feelinglessness that had fallen on her like a sudden fog after her mother's body had been driven down the road to Yauco. No pain. It was rare for her to feel no pain. She wasn't going to risk its return, however much the neighbors disapproved.

Rebecca didn't go because she'd seen what they had done to her father in New York. They had put him in a metal lined coffin, put the coffin in a large cement box set in a large hole in the cemetery grounds and, after the family left, lowered a large cement lid on the box before scooping the earth back over it. Stored in the ground like pemmican—that's what some Native American had once said about the way the non-Indian people preserved their dead from decay. As if they were saving them up for a famine year. She wanted Pepa laid under her banana plants, to rot along with the leaves and overripe fruit, fertilizing the garden she'd dug and cleaned of weeds with her stumpy machete, filed short over the years.

So Rebecca stayed home and sorted out "el mess" as Esther had called it. On the bed were three cartons full of things Anselma had always yearned to throw away, except that Pepa wouldn't let her: old clippings, large numbers of empty medicine vials, ancient greeting cards, ball-point pens that didn't write, indecipherable letters from Medicare, the boxes gifts came in, especially the little ones, and pencil stubs. Pepa never threw away a pencil no matter how short it got. Rebecca was tossing yet another of those omnipresent vials when she saw something through its brown translucent plastic sides. She recovered the vial from the trash bag and shook it. She heard and felt nothing but when she opened it, there they were, small tight rolls like green suppositories. She didn't realize right away what they were except that they looked like paper, but when she pulled the top one out and unrolled it she caught sight of the number 100 in one of the corners. There were two of them, two one hundred dollar bills folded lengthwise then rolled into a tube that resisted unwrapping and under them four more tubes were tightly wedged. Maria walked in just then and sent Rebecca such a look of deep suspicion that Rebecca felt guilty as she explained. Maria sat right down on the bed next to her while Rebecca emptied out the garbage bag between them and laboriously they opened each resistant childproof cap clamped stubbornly to its vial. In the end they found three that were filled with money, one thousand and ten dollars between them. Maria smoothed out the bills one by one and patted them like cats on her lap and finally slipped them all into the plastic drugstore bag she had thrown away earlier.

Maria wanted that money. For herself. Not just because she could use the money but because she deserved it, because her mother owed it to her. She'd been given so little—so little love, so little anything else, forgetting, as she always did, that Pepa had raised Maria's son for her after she'd lost her tiny little daughter two hours after she was born. Her doll of a daughter, with long black hair almost to her eyebrows and a sweet soft mouth gasping for air. In her despair she couldn't bear to touch her two year old boy. Pepa took in the bewildered and sorrowing Rafael and kept him for 11 years, and she gave him the affection and instruction she had never given any of her own. Pepa had considered not returning him when Maria finally asked for him back, but the boy deserved better schools and his father was making good money in New York. Rafael didn't

want to go, but he went where he was sent, reluctant and sulky, afraid to look as angry as he felt. But he returned every summer to his beloved grandmother's farm while his mother and father took a cabin in Connecticut and fought each other silently and savagely, freed from the necessity of taking him into consideration. In the end those two lost him totally because his daydreams about them, the stories he'd made up in his younger years to console himself, were no longer believable. He was his grandmother's boy and accepted it, and Maria resented it and denied it at one and the same time.

Maria, her hands wringing the bag with the money, for once said what she meant—that the old wooden house was a festering sore, that now that her mother was dead she would have it torn down gladly and without delay. Anselma could see the bitter triumph on Maria's face and it gave her strength. She threw back the covers and struggled dizzily out of bed, her face stiff with anger, to lean over the seated Maria. Anselma's nightgown tangled around her legs and fluttered in the wind from the storm that was blowing off the Caribbean. She looked frightening, her usually calm eyes starting out like boiled eggs, her twisted mouth saying that Maria would go to hell, burn down there for eternity like a morcilla left to fry too long in the pan; that long before that, she, Anselma, would see to it that everyone knew every single dishonorable, shameful thing Maria had ever done, everything Pepa had told her in the long evening hours they shared day after day for years. She would give Maria a migraine worse than any she had ever complained of, a migraine that would make her incapable of eating, walking or pissing, incapable of even taking her miserable stupid pills. She told Maria to leave, to take the miserable, maldito money, to get out and stay out, never to show her cara de culo in Indiera any more. Maria slipped from her chair and stood hiding behind it, stepped back as Anselma advanced, back until she reached the door and turned and ran, tripping over the cat and saving herself by grabbing for the porch rail and upsetting an aloe plant in its clay pot, shattering it on the tile floor. But Maria didn't notice.

She was sobbing into the wind, running down the dirt road as she had run more times than she could count, all through her unbearable childhood. Fry in hell? Anselma and Pepa would be the ones to fry in hell. Those witches. They deserved to die in this hole. Right then, while she slipped and recovered her balance on the red mud, she decided at long last to leave. No force on earth could keep her on this godforsaken island anymore. She had been a fool to have returned, a fool not to have left again long ago. Her mother had poisoned every single bit of this place, all the way across the thirty-five by one hundred and eleven miles of it and every Puerto Rican soul that ever lived. She would go to Cincinnati to her friend Lucy, a good Scotch Irish French German American who thought Puerto Rico was a brand of cigars. Anselma could keep her pieces of rotten wood. She could keep her dirty money. But she clutched the little bag in her fist as she ran.

In Anselma's bedroom, Mercedita's slippers slapped softly as she moved from the bureau to the bed with the last dose of antibiotics of the day. In the kitchen Rebecca was brewing yerba buena, one of the herbs Anselma insisted on. Mercedita moved with self-conscious care, imagining herself in a large city hospital, moving from bed to bed. Anselma must be a cancer patient. No. She was about to be operated on for a damaged heart valve. Mercedita's nursing would save her life.

Anselma didn't know any of that, she only knew that Mercedita's hand was cool and kind, her voice soft, her smile reassuring. She would have made a good nurse. In a year she would be out of high school, but where was there money for nursing school? Her mother was useless, always sick and crabby, and her father earned only enough to keep them from debt. Pobrecita. If only Anselma could discover what Pepa had done with that money. It was a lot of money. It had to be. Manuel sent checks regularly. She knew, she gave them to Carlos to cash in town, not in the store by the road. You didn't want everyone in the neighborhood to know you had that much money. Pepa hid the bills behind her bed and spent very little of it. She knew, she did the shopping for them both. The soft rolls Pepa presented to Juancito, slipped to Elena, hadn't made a dent in the bulky envelopes she dipped into. But now? At least what was left, what Anselma's fingertips had reached, deep in the narrow pocket between the room added on twenty years ago and the old cabin, could help a little. "Un poco," she muttered with disdain. What good would a little do?

It was in a thin rasp of a voice that Anselma refused her tea and ordered the two girls—Ay they were young!—to sit and listen.

Mercedita took it calmly, both the promise of money and its loss. But then she'd always known Pepa would do what she could. Help would be wonderful but she would be a nurse somehow or other, with or without Pepa's money. But Rebecca was flabbergasted. When she had told Pepa about her dream to quit her job and paint for a year or, why not? two years, it was only because Pepa loved her paintings, shone with pride at her ability to make the beauty of Pepa's world public. It was as if Rebecca read her mind, as if she looked through Pepa's eyes at the rough gray-brown texture of the old wood and the earth-red, worn roof against the smooth grass-green shine of a new banana leaf and published it on paper and canvas.

Rebecca couldn't take Pepa's money. Not possibly. Rebecca owned a car, even if it was eight years old, a television, a VCR. She was rich compared to Pepa. It was madness.

But not to Anselma. Slowly, sipping the minty brew Mercedita pressed on her every few sentences to ease the raw swelling in her throat, she explained just how much money Pepa had saved and for whom and for what and why she had hidden it behind her bed. They were shocked. Mercedita because she'd never heard of that much money, thousands and thousands, in the hands of anyone she knew. Celebrities, maybe, or big lottery winners or corrupt government officials headlined on the front page of El Vocero, had money like that. Rebecca because her jíbara great-grandmother, the one who lived, fully and happily to be sure, on guineos and bacalao in a wood cabin without running water, who bathed in a tin tub and depended on an outhouse no one else in the family deigned to use, had more money to give her than her mother's retired accountant father.

Once had. The money was gone. Hidden away from Anselma's watchful eyes. How? Pepa had been sick for months, lying day after day in a darkened room, waving Anselma away, refusing help even to get to the outhouse, all those weeks she had had that incessant diarrhea. She didn't throw it away. Anselma would have found It. Did she eat it? Is that why her intestines were protesting? If not that, then what? Where could it have gone?

"¡Buscalo!" commanded Anselma in her fading voice, an Anselma suddenly full of urgency and strength.. She couldn't bear it if Pepa's money didn't get to the people she'd hoarded it for. "Find it. En secreto. The way Pepa wanted it. She wanted it for you, not for that ingrata of a Maria. For your schooling," she told Mercedita. "For your paintings," she said to Rebecca who sat in a trance staring at the pattern of Anselma's nightgown, daisies, roses, delphiniums, day lilies in miniature bunches repeated up and down the length of it. When Rebecca's tears began to fall, blurring the pattern, one drop, then another, then sheets of them wetting her face, Anselma gave in at last to the pain in her heart, hid her face in the waiting pillow and began to sob out the sorrow that would last her for what was left of her life. Mercedita, slumped against the bureau, the teacup still in her hands, howled her loneliness for the only real mother she had ever known. When Esther returned from the store she heard them and coming to stand in the doorway, grocery bag against her breast, cried too.

In the end they found only $1,800 more. There was $628 behind Pepa's bed, the rest in other hiding places: under the lining of her underwear drawer, in a medicine vial on the shelf with her aspirins and cough medicine, in one of her shoes. They brought the bills to Anselma and counted them on her bed. There was one bill with a heart on it and crossing herself first, then swearing them to secrecy, Anselma told them about the abortion—que Dios la perdone—and how two years later, " la muchacha" whom she wouldn't name, had begun paying back the bank, as she called it. Pepa had taken only that one bill, the marked one, and sent the rest back for her to start un sucursal, a branch office.

Out of the blue she added, "Pepa didn't want to die, you know. But she was going to. She knew it." And she told again the stories of her gifts, the money she had given Doña Fela's cousin-in-law to pay the fine the time when he was taken to court and found guilty of trespassing on his landlord's porch when he went to complain about the leaking roof. About how important it was to her that Mercedita study nursing. And how Pepa had become suspicious at the end.

Rebecca listened to the scratchy voice, Anselma's love for Pepa in every word. But where was Pepa's love for Anselma? Was it only humility that the stories she told were of Pepa's love for Elena, Juancito, Rebecca, Mercedita? Anselma openly regretted Pepa's secretiveness but was she inwardly regretting more—that Pepa's best feelings were for her chicks not for the woman at her side, the comrade of her last years.

The picture Rebecca had begun in her head, the one she would paint in the month she could take off from work with her share of the money they had found, had begun to alter almost without Rebecca noticing. As she nursed Anselma, helped Esther with the chickens, gathered herbs, bananas, and cabbage from the garden for Mercedita to carry back to Ponce with her, she roughed in another figure in the painting she was composing in her mind. It appeared beside the coffee tree she had imagined growing out of a hole in the kitchen floor by the sink. Pepa's form already stood sketched into the middle of the kitchen reaching up to hold the flower end of a bunch of bananas with one hand, her machete in the other slicing up to cut the thick stem growing out from a cluster of shredded banana leaves. Anselma's figure took shape across from Pepa's. She was filtering tinta de café through the coffee-stained colador, the brown liquid flowing out of the bulging cloth bag and down her legs in rivulets to the small rock-strewn river flowing between her feet, past the roots of the banana, between Pepa's toes and out the wide open kitchen door. Out there beyond the trees was the city, perhaps San Juan, or Honolulu or Munich or New York

It wasn't much, 900 dollars, but Rebecca agreed with Anselma and Esther, and with Mercedita who would not accept more than her share, that she had to use it as Pepa intended. With her own small savings and the rest of her vacation time she could paint uninterrupted for four to five weeks. She sketched every moment she could, sketched Anselma's face, the garden, chickens seen through the holes in the floor, pecking under the house.

Mercedita was leaving tomorrow. She had missed too much school already, otherwise she would have stayed and left with Esther and Rebecca the following Monday. Rebecca had also missed too much work, but she'd called the office and returned immediately to her journal, drawing each wind-carved board of the outhouse wall in painstaking detail.

Pepa's gift—the one she had intended, as well as the present more modest one—left Esther's mind in a knot of contradictions. On the one hand she thought Rebecca's middle class guilt and her notions about Pepa's poverty were silly. Esther had no patience with them. Of course Rebecca should join Mercedita and look for the rest of the money and keep her half if she found it.

But I couldn't do what Pepa did. I didn't take out any of my money for Rebecca's year off. I don't offer it even now. I want my daughter to take care of herself, not depend on someone else to pay for her daily bread and her ice cream on Sundays. "And if painting can't guarantee you week in, week out, food and drink, my girl" she had once told her, "then keep it for the weekend." Esther didn't want it all handed to Rebecca, didn't want her swamped by the color televisions and leather coats her own parents wrapped their affection in.

But it pained her to see the intense absorption with which Becca went about fulfilling her own and Pepa's dream for her. The calm joy of it. For the first time she saw her daughter's constant drawing not as self-indulgent play, as a luxury, but as work. She felt she had been stingy, hard, unloving. She felt the way she'd felt when Rafael had criticized her for her anger at her father's birthday checks.

"He's giving you what he never had."

"But I don't want money from him! "she had shouted.

"So what!" he'd shouted back , "He loves you, dammit."

She thought of Maria clutching the plastic bag with Pepa's money in it as she ran. Is it money, is that what makes us all so crazy? Or are we all stupid, wrong and stupid, about our own children?

"Shit!" Rebecca spat out the word as she made a useless grab at the damned vial.

She had spotted it in the rafters of the outhouse while she was sketching the mango tree behind it, and standing on tiptoe, had reached for it and toppled it with her fingertip. It had rolled through the hole in seat which she'd left uncovered. She was very annoyed with herself. She needed to know if it had any money in it and look where it had ended! Well, here goes, she thought, holding her breath even though the overpowering stench was of the Pine Sol which Pepa, and now Rebecca, poured in after each use.

Too dark to see. In a bad temper Rebecca stomped off to the kitchen where she had caught sight of a flashlight. As she trudged back she heard her mother calling that Mercedita was ready to leave. "In a minute," she shouted back. The faint beam caught the uncapped vial but wasn't strong enough to penetrate the brown plastic. With a sour face Rebecca looked around for something to poke that vial out with. When she turned the flashlight back into the hole it caught something white on the back panel of the privy bench. A thick cord running arrow straight from a nail down into the muck. And further on, another. Four altogether. She could hear Esther and Mercedita in the kitchen and knew she had to hurry. Only she had this growing suspicion she had to examine. Now! Before Mercedita left. It wasn't possible, was it? Pepa couldn't have done what she was imagining she'd done, could she? With her body in an awkward twist, her nostrils pinched against the Pine Sol and the whiff of something less pleasant underneath, she pulled cautiously at the nearest cord. It was heavy. Weighted, maybe. And just before she reached the part of the string that had been buried and soiled, the top of a bag tied to the end of the string broke the surface—a clear plastic bag bulging with the shapes of many, many, many vials.

She sat back on her heels with a look of blank astonishment on her face. Pepa, sick weak Pepa had done this. Diarrhea, my eye! Wily Pepa. I bet she was thinking about how fastidious Maria is and how she—and Manuel—never step in here. Rebecca giggled. She thought of telling Anselma, cleanly Anselma, or her own squeamish mother. She laughed out loud. The more she thought of it the funnier it seemed.

"Buried treasure!" she whooped, thinking of the stinking bag of vials. Her laughter gurgled out of her, her belly shook. She leaned against the privy door and laughed and laughed. Her mother came running up and stopped at the sight of her daughter convulsed with laughter. Mercedita was waiting and anyway what was there to laugh about? It made Esther nervous and angry to watch Rebecca going hysterical like this without rhyme or reason. Her mother's serious face made the whole situation even funnier for Rebecca, who was trying to stop so she could tell her what she'd found, but all she did was laugh that much harder so that tears came to her eyes. It wasn't really that funny, she told herself, but she couldn't stop. She looked up for something to distract her from the funniness of everything. Through her wet eyes, past her mother's worried face, she saw the scene from the doorway of Pepa's outhouse like a crayon sketch for one of her own paintings: the dark green shadow of the trees, the darker path between them. Then the kitchen door in the morning light and Mercedita in it, dressed in a white skirt and blouse. On her feet, worn sneakers for the walk down the red mud path to the road. A handbag on her shoulder, her town shoes in her hand.

Jane Speed, Aurora Levins Morales &
Rosario Morales (lying down.) August 1954

Forget Me Not

*In a small lichen stained cemetery at the meeting of the Lares and Yau-
co roads, two remarkable women from Alabama lie buried. Jane Speed
and her mother Mary (Maga) Craik Speed, also known as Dolly, were
wealthy southern aristocrats turned communist. In the 1930s Jane ran
a radical bookstore in Birmingham that was one of the few places where
Black and white radicals could meet to talk about ideas and socialize. In
1939, Jane married César Andreu Iglesias, a Puerto Rican communist
journalist and labor organizer, and, with her mother, moved to Puerto
Rico. In 1951, my parents, also communists, moved to the island from
New York, and became close friends with Jane and her family. My parents bought the farm in the western mountains of the island where I was
born. Later the Speed-Andreu family built a house on my parents' land,
just up the hill from ours. When I was two, my parents returned to New
York while my father went to graduate school. Three years later, Jane died*

suddenly of a stroke, and the rest of the family left the farm and moved to San Juan.

I don't remember Jane, and have only one clear memory of her mother, but from the age of six, I grew up in the house they had built, surrounded by their stories, things they had owned, traditions they had started, like Sunday afternoon tea to the sound of Gilbert and Sullivan operettas, played on their old Victrola. I absorbed the tales of their boldness, the civil disobedience, the illegal flag, sewn by hand, but as a child who lived outdoors as much as possible, in that continually changing tropical landscape, their most tangible legacy was the endurance of their gardens. Dahlias that popped up in the tomato bed, elegant white and peach colored gladioli thrusting up thick stalks at the edge of a path, clumps of pale blue forget-me-nots creeping up over stones in the little clearing between the lime trees where we had planted strawberries—and the great spilling torrent of bloom of the bougainvillea, jasmine and honeysuckle that poured off the tin roof.

This story is not about Jane and Maga, but they were in my mind. They were such vivid women that their ghosts still inhabit the people and places they touched. I have borrowed details from their lives: Jane's magnificent red hair and presence of mind, Maga's sharp tongue and eyes, their Southernness and radicalism and their passion for flowers. But once I had done so, a simple disclaimer would no longer do.

Agnes and Martha are characters of fiction, and the feelings I attribute to them come purely from the wild interior of my own mind. The people in this story are made up. Raúl is not César. The garden is not their garden, but it grew from the imagination of a child who wandered in the ruins of what they planted. Imagination run riot, blooming over and around the tiny pebbles of fact. So this is not their story. Nevertheless, in my fictions, I pay them homage.

She had hair the color of old flamboyán petals, when they've fallen to the road and been quenched from flame to a glowing orange, and it fell, when it was loose, nearly twenty pounds of it, to the backs of her knees. But most of the time it coiled around her head in a heavy, shining braid. The girl, Chela, had once seen her washing it, the white foam of the soap and the red strands turning dark in the cold water. Cold water brought out the shine of hair, Agnes believed, and she always washed it by dipping a saucepan in one of the tin buckets she had lifted up from the mossy cistern. Once she had washed in steaming water that poured from gilded faucets into a gleaming porcelain tub. She had had scented soaps from England, lavender and rose and honeysuckle, piles of soft white towels, and vases full of fresh flowers always standing on her dresser. Dark-skinned women had moved through her father's house carrying piles of clothing which was always pressed and fresh and ready for her to wear. Now she ladled cold water over her head, leaning forward in an old cotton dress at the edge of a thicket of wild ginger. The soapy run-off trickled into a mat of wild mint, and its pungent odor rose in the tropical morning, from where she had crushed it underfoot with her thick-soled outdoor shoes.

Raúl had brought her here. For that she was still grateful. A fiery opposition journalist with a mobile olive face, flashing black eyes and expressive hands, he had swept her off her feet. They had met at a convention on rural organizing. Agnes and her mother Martha had taken the train up from New Orleans, leaving the bookstore in the charge of Agnes' assistant. There had been a week of crowded rooms, intense debate, talk until all hours of the night, and Raúl. She had been delighted with his intensity, his flair, his convictions. He had wooed her with skill and persistence, talked movingly about his captive country, made passionate love to her in the early morning hours after the meetings were over, and openly exulted at winning her. She had fallen hard, she admitted. She had packed up her most essential belongings, and come, with her mother, to the island. She had tried to sell the bookstore to her assistant, but Daniel had gently refused. He would keep it for her for a while, he'd said.

The affair with Raul had lasted nearly a year, which, now that she had known him for so long, she thought remarkable. But when it became clear that his consuming passion was for beginning relationships, the headiness of courtship as addicting to him as whisky had been to Agnes' father, and she had found herself once more single, in a foreign country whose language she spoke only haltingly, she had been surprised to discover in herself no desire to go home. Some time during that year she had fallen in love, deeply and irrevocably, with the new life she was living. Turning to retrace her steps, she had found, to her relief, that her bridges were all burned.

They had lived together, Raúl, Agnes and Martha, in a small house in the mountains. The last few months of the affair had been tense, Raúl alternately sulky and caressing, Agnes heartsick, literally, with a dull throbbing ache in her chest that the drops her doctor in New Orleans had sent her did little to ease, and Martha with her bristling white wisps of hair, brilliant blue jay's eyes, and sharp, economical tongue, snorting at the two of them over her glasses. "Randy as a tomcat, Aggy. Ought to shoot him."

Raúl had moved out, and after a few more months he had stopped coming at odd hours trying to coax her back, and they had had peace. It was then she had found out how much she loved it here: the candlelit nights with rain drumming on the roof; the moist mornings, fragrant with lemon flowers and drenched in tropical light; air so clear you could hear a bucket clanking against a stone on the next mountain, and these people. They reminded her of sharecropping families back home, the women with their eight or ten thin children, their cotton dresses, weathered faces and drooping breasts. The men clustered at a wooden counter under one bare bulb, drinking rum after a long day planting bananas for one of the Pachecos.

But here she was not their hereditary oppressor, Judge Johnson's granddaughter, always having to push her way through generations of resentful deference. Here she was only a peculiar foreign woman who had lived in the old green house up the hill as *la mujer de Raúl Santos* who had moved on and was now sleeping with that blonde schoolteacher in Yagrumo. In their quick-tongued rural Spanish, to which she could only haltingly respond, the women of Candelarias extended to her a kind of cautious welcome out of their common condition as women, gave her the names of their children, small gifts of food, and asked for bitter orange leaves from her trees to doctor their stomach aches. She was still a gringa with a house full of books, but she had no ownership in the economy that shaped their lives. For the first time she was free of that refused inheritance. The shadow of the great white house no longer fell across her conversations.

Raúl had turned out, after a decent interval, to be a much better co-agitator than lover. For the past ten years they had worked together on and off: she and Raúl, Paco and Elena who went back and forth between a house in Yagrumo and Paco's mother's home in Ponce, and recently Alfonso, an earnest botany student from Mayagüez, and Estela and her Jewish husband Reuben, both from New York. Every few weeks they met in the sala of the small green house Agnes had bought from Raúl with the money she got from selling the bookstore to Daniel. The rest of the time it was just the two of them, Agnes and Martha, and now the child, Graciela.

Nothing could have seemed more unlikely than that Graciela, thin, unpretty, painfully shy, should have ventured close enough to the eccentric Americana to see her, let alone attract her attention. Tacha, Chela's busy, outspoken, bustling aunt didn't know where the girl was half the time, always slipping away into the monte and coming back with twigs of unknown plants. It was the flowers that had started it.

One afternoon she had slid along the slope below Agnes' house, picking her way into the long abandoned bitter orange grove where she hoped to find some of those silky green orchids that sometimes grew from the clefts of old trees. It had been a cool day, and Agnes, scorning the sunhat her fair skin usually required her to wear outdoors, had been fertilizing the roses, sweet, white, old fashioned climbing roses grown from a cutting she had taken on a visit to her old home. The girl had never come this close to the house before, and her first glimpse of the roses, cascading down the rough trellis Agnes and Martha had erected, stopped her in her tracks and caused her to gasp. A small, animal sound, but Agnes heard it.

Agnes' Spanish was still heavily accented, not with the Brooklyn Yiddish curl of Reuben's, but with a kind of twangy twist to her vowels, those Louisiana diphthongs washed with a faint tinting of French. She was completely fluent by now. She could argue about nationalism in a cadre meeting and negotiate the price of a hen, but she did not, at first, know how to talk flowers with this child who crept up out of the massed greenery of the abandoned citrus grove to touch the creamy petals of her roses. After all, there is nothing so personal, so provincial, so particular to your own patch of earth as the names of flowers. The bougainvillea that she had grown up seeing on the garden walls of her aunts' homes in Baton Rouge, was known here as *trinitaria*, for the trinity of fuchsia leaves clustered around the tiny poky flower. Coleus, with its distinguished looking purple and green foliage suitable for borders, stood blushing in wild thickets or transplanted into rusted cracker cans, and was called *vergüenza,* meaning shame or embarrassment.

But they had managed. They had spent the afternoon moving from one side of the house to the other, looking into the hearts of spider lilies with their overpowering perfume, brilliant tiger lilies, stately amaryllis, tall gladioli, white throated and dusted with purple and gold, red dahlias and pink zinnias, the bush roses, dark red and pale yellow, the fall of starry jasmine, and in the back, the herbs, the strawberry bed, and the tiny blue forget-me-nots.

Graciela began to come every day after school. Agnes turned her loose with a trowel, gave her bulbs to plant, and let her putter to..."her heart's content," thought Agnes, watching the glow of happiness and confidence on the child's face as she crouched over the red earth she was digging. One rainy day Agnes called her in and made her ginger tea, and gave her the Guide to Exotic Flowers to look at. Soon she was sitting beside her, pointing out flowers she had seen and asking the girl what they were called. That was the day she discovered that Graciela couldn't read. Not just badly, as most children schooled casually in this community of farm laborers did, but not at all.

That night, as the rain pounded on the tin roof she thought long and hard. Then she went to her mother's room to consult with her. Martha did not like small children, nor did she, after a dozen years of residing, as she put it, in a Gaugin painting, speak the language of the place that was her home. She saw no need. But she did not approve of neglect, and she was a passionate gardener. Indeed, the hardest thing about leaving her autocratic, hard drinking bully of a husband had been the knowledge that her gardens, the brilliant and fragrant cutting garden in the back, and the display gardens, with their formal beds, would undoubtedly be neglected, maybe even uprooted in the wake of her departure. Her sister-in-law, who had taken charge of keeping house, favored smooth lawns and a few showy shrubs. So in the end she agreed to Agnes' proposal, and the next day Agnes walked over to pay a call on Graciela's aunt.

It turned out to be surprisingly easy. The aunt was the harassed mother of six other children, five of them still at home. She had a genuine if casual affection for the child, and Agnes' offer satisfied her from both points of view. She would have settled it all right then, but Agnes insisted that Graciela be asked, and be given a day or two to think it over. This seemed a mad excess of delicacy to the aunt, but she shrugged. If you were rich and Americana you could afford excess. The next morning early, Agnes stepped out to gather a few of the blue forget-me-nots to put on the breakfast table. She loved their cool, temperate color. It made a refreshing change, sometimes, from the flame reds, sizzling pinks and purples, the deep yellows and steamy greens. There, sitting under the lemon tree, was Graciela.

She had hardly slept from excitement, nervousness, and a helpless gazing at approaching change: grown people, gente mayor, decided children's lives the way tía decided which chicken to kill for sopita. Even the good changes were out of your hands. She had sat under the lemon tree, watching light spilling across the garden, trying to understand that this was now to be her house. She would have good clothes, her aunt had explained, and the Americanas would teach her, and if she wanted, send her to la high in Yagrumo when she was older. This, her aunt explained, was her great good luck. She must be careful to behave well, and help out as much as she could, so they didn't change their minds. But looking up at Agnes watching her she suddenly thought, "Tía doesn't understand. It's not like that at all." Agnes smiled at her, and bent to pick the little blue ones. Suddenly Graciela felt like skipping.

Rain fell heavily, in great skeins of water, like hanks of silky transparent rope. Like hair falling from the clouds. Chela watched fat drops striking the narrow petals of the spider lilies that sprang back after each blow. She was tired. She had gotten up before dawn to drive the four hours from San Juan, passing the white cliff faces of Lares limestone at around eight, as the sun broke golden over the cordillera and flooded the narrow little valleys through which the road climbed. Now, as she sat by the window, her mind was full of flowers—all the flowers she and Agnes had planted, watered, cut back, harvested for bouquets to fill the little house with scent and color, that she had cut again this morning to heap on the raw red earth of Agnes' grave. She turned and looked behind her. At the other window, Martha sat, staring grimly out. Chela went and stood beside her. Martha reached out and took her hand and squeezed it hard in a rare gesture.

"Te vienes conmigo. You're coming home with me." said Chela.

"I won't." Martha spat back.

"You will, if I have to tie you up, you damned stubborn old woman."

Martha glanced up at her with an appreciative flash of humor in her eyes. But she still looked, thought Graciela, as if she'd been struck by lightening. She remembered the time the house had been hit, when she was sixteen. It rippled down the cables that the jasmine climbed, and the smell of burnt flowers had stayed by that corner of the house for weeks. Now, seeing the look in Martha's eyes, Graciela finally began to cry, and after a moment Martha pulled her down into the rocker beside her. As Graciela sobbed in great shudders, her head sank into Martha's lap, and the old woman stroked her hair, saying "Hush, child, don't take on so," while the tears ran down her own wrinkled face.

Five and a half years later, she came back to bury Martha next to Agnes. She was the head nurse, now, and it was harder to get away, but she had some sick days left, and she took them. Martha's would be the last grave in the little cemetery. It was old and crowded, and the walls were in disrepair, but Martha had disdained the smooth lawns and white gravel paths of Cementerio las Palmas near the small house they shared in the capital. Here her bones would be wrapped in roots that pried apart her coffin, her grave inundated in wild grass and those little white daisy-like weeds, an untidiness she had never tolerated in life. After the burial, Chela sat at a table in the tiny cafetín down the road, struggling with her English, and wrote a letter to the surviving nephew, a prosperous lawyer in New Orleans. She sealed it, and gave it to Toño to give to the mail car when it came through, with two coins for the stamp. Then she walked up the path to the green house.

It was dimmed by years of mildew and the lack of Martha's eagle eye, directing some neighborhood boy with a soapy brush to scrub off every black stain. The paint had faded, too. Under it, the pale brown wood showed in places. The yellow rose had been swallowed by hibiscus and señorita. The spider lilies were drowned in grass, and the creamy white roses that had first drawn her here were choked in dead leaves and withered blossoms. She walked slowly, sadly around to the back. Who would have guessed it had been a garden. In the country, you couldn't turn your back on anything you planted. The monte ate it up. She felt a bad-tempered panic. She couldn't make the journey from the city, and there was no one here who cared. Already vandals had broken windows and leaning in she could see the electric pump the women had gotten the last year before Agnes' death was gone, ripped out, with the loose wires left dangling. There were no bulbs in the sockets.

After a moment she waded out into the grass. The edges of the blades scraped her legs, ruining her stockings. Then a flash of color drew her eye. Spread out in a spongy carpet between the roots of the limes, tangled with the wiry stems of grass, creeping into the shade under the ranks of hibiscus were tiny blue flowers, pale under the tropical sky, but gone wild now, able to sustain themselves without human aid. Forget-me-nots, making a small garden where no one ever came any more.

Graciela remembered the day Agnes had shown them to her. "I missed them, you see," she had said smiling down at them. Now that she looked, she could see a gladiolus, over there, under the low boughs of the pine that had spread wider and wider over the years. The tree should be cut back. It should be cut back and its tip pruned so it would fill out, and not grow straggly. The yellow roses should be untangled from the bushes and vines that always grew back so fast, tied back onto the trellis, the dead flowers plucked from the white roses, the gladioli bulbs separated and replanted, the house cleaned and set in order. But no one would.

Now that it was hers, Pancho would want to buy the strip by the road for more coffee, and Chago, on the other side, would certainly have moved the fence several times since Martha had gone away. People wanted visible use. Houses, market crops, pigpens and chicken coops. They would tell her to sell it, and she would put it off, letting the lichen stained pomarosas bear their perfumed fruit in peace. She stood in the sweet scent of the ruined roses, listening to the cuckoos in the valley announcing rain, and then she turned and walked swiftly back to the road where she had left her car.

The letter came on a Thursday, three years later. Ani, Reuben and Estela's daughter, writing from California. Chela barely remembered them. They had left not long after she had come, taking their fat, dark-eyed baby with the mop of black hair in her eyes to some faraway city where Reuben had a job. Only Estela had come for Agnes' funeral. By the time they moved back to the island, Chela had been at nursing school in the capital and the family had settled in Mayagüez. She'd only seen the child once, lanky and blonde by then. Ani was a writer, she said. She had a fellowship. Could she stay in the house for a few months? She knew it was in bad repair. But she had been a carpenter, too, out there in San Francisco. She would make it habitable in exchange.

Rain pattered on the tin roof. Ani knew it would be pounding soon. She had spent five days with buckets of soapy water and a hard bristled brush, scouring neglect from walls and tiles, cutting out rotted counters and shelving, removing splinters of windowpane. The wiring had been "harvested," so she bought a kerosene quinqué and a box of candles. Miraculously, the stove was intact, and tomorrow the men would deliver a tank of gas. She'd found the old kitchen table on its side, one leg broken, dragged it to the room that faced north, and used a bracket from a worm eaten shelf to fasten it to the wall, under one of the few windows that was unbroken. She had hired Paquito Velez to repair and put up the old hurricane shutters until she could order glass cut and delivered from town.

Waves of rain swept across the hills, turning the green leaves of the yagrumos silver side up, and dashed themselves against the crest of mountain where the house stood. Bushes whipped against the house, tapped and scraped at the walls. The afternoon was darkening toward dusk and her body ached, but she felt stories batting at her like moths against the window, seeking the yellow flare of the quinque. The wick was too long and it was smoking. She trimmed it, then sat down at the table on a borrowed chair.

She had set out her old manual typewriter, a small blue portable she'd dug out of the attic, and a stack of clean white pages. Somewhere in a damp corner under the sink, a single coquí called from the dark, its sweet liquid notes rising above the chorus of frogs and crickets outside. She thought of all the others who had lived here since Raúl's father had had it built in the 1920s, people she had seen in curled black and white photographs, stacked in envelopes by year, and the first color snapshots, aging into unlikely greens and oranges. Her parents, younger than she could remember them, Martha, stiffly holding her infant self, and Agnes, who had been her mother's dear friend. She had imagined that life so intensely, those vivid years fallen into the leaf litter of the past, long before

her own childhood visits, driving up from the coast into the smell of rain, fermenting coffee beans, and fresh bread. The layers of it has settled into her, leaves and flowers, snail shells and lizard bones, conversations from which the words had evaporated, and people who lived only in the thin emulsion of old photographs, compacted into her personal soil. She had swept out a drift of decaying petals and pine needles from the south bedroom, well on its way to becoming earth, in which a few minute seedlings had already sprouted. Well, she had come here to unearth the mysteries of memory, to dig in the neglected burial ground of her inheritance, to water these lost seeds and make them bloom.

She pulled the typewriter closer. The swift dark had fallen, and the lamp light caught at drops of water driven against the glass and made them spark like fireflies. She rolled the first sheet of paper into place. Slowly the inner quiet she had summoned settled around her. The dark was full of whispers and rustlings, and the endless downpour of years, striking tin and flowing away, down the mountains of the cordillera, toward the sea, drenching her imagination. She began to type. *She had hair the color of old flamboyán petals*, she wrote, *when they've fallen to the road.*

Fin

Also by Aurora Levins Morales

Kindling: Writings on the Body
(Palabrera Press, 2013)

This new collection of poetry and prose explores the body as a site of pleasure, pain and political struggle. Disabled and chronically ill writer, historian and activist Aurora Levins Morales writes about epilepsy and stroke, the social control of dark skinned women's sexuality and the erotics of chronic fatigue, epigenetics and healing justice, community based science and what it's like to get health care in Cuba. In lushly poetic prose, Levins Morales bridges the gap between the intimately personal and the global, between sensual experience and visionary theory.

"Aurora's writing is itself a kind of alchemy, balancing emotional nuance with rich historical context, simultaneously speaking in an intimate, personal voice and for a collective we. She offers us vulnerable, power-filled lyricism that moves the audience to new understandings of their own lives, as she claims her body's pleasure and pain."

Patty Berne, Co-founder and Artistic Director, *Sins Invalid.*

Telling To Live: Latina Feminist Testimonios

by The Latina Feminist Group
(Duke University Press, 2001)

"Telling to Live may be one of the most important books published in the last few decades. Latinas collectively have not had a book like this before that features so many different backgrounds and cultures...The inclusion of all these mix-and-match identifications is what makes this book required reading in women's studies classes all across the globe."

—Jocelyn Climent, in *Bust*

Remedios: Stories of Earth and Iron from the History of Puertorriqueñas

(Beacon Press, 1998, South End Press, 2001)

"Captivating language and enticing cadence are characteristics of the enchanting prose Levins Morales employs in this gathering of uniquely realized vignettes...Exciting melange of stories ultimately affirming the empowerment of women."

— Booklist

"There is no other book like Remedios. It is history, anthropology, poetry, and myth; it is a song and a prayer. Aurora Levins Morales is a Jewish Latina curandera who embraces diverse legacies with passion and eloquence. In stories so beautifully told they soar off the page...she offers us remedies that heal our bodies and souls and feed our spirits of our many forgotten ancestors."

—Ruth Behar, author of *The Vulnerable Observer*

Medicine Stories

South End Press, 1998

In Medicine Stories, Levins Morales writes lucidly about the complexities of social identity and radical activism. Her lyrical meditations on ecology, children's liberation, sexuality, and history show how political transformation and personal healing are inextricably bound. Levins Morales is a survivor of childhood sexual abuse and was raised as a Jewish "red diaper baby" in the mountains of Puerto Rico.

At the heart of this book is the conviction that our survival depends on crafting a political practice capable of healing all our wounds, from global, macro-economic injustices to the intimate scars of cruelty in our own lives.

Getting Home Alive (with Rosario Morales)

(Firebrand Books, 1986)

Revised & Expanded Edition coming in 2014 from Palabrera Press

This mother–daughter, mixed genre collaboration was hailed as "a landmark in US Puerto Rican literature" and "the most important book to come out of the diaspora in a generation," a call and response across generations, migration and languages.

"Serious, literary and passionate." — Publisher's Weekly

Coming Soon
from Palabrera Press
www.palabrerapress.com

Poet On Assignment

Following 9/11 Aurora Levins Morales' poem "Shema" went viral. It was repeatedly broadcast on Pacifica radio, and read at dozens of anti-war demonstrations nationwide. During the following months, Aurora was hired by Pacifica's Flashpoints news magazine to write poetry commentaries on the news. Poet On Assignment collects these "rapid response poems" for the first time.

Signal Series #1

De Rebelde A Revolucionario/ From Rebel to Revolutionary

by Richard Levins

Written during a critical moment in the Puerto Rican struggle for independence, this influential 1966 essay has enduring lessons for the radicals of today. This new, bilingual edition includes an introductory essay and historical notes.

CPSIA information can be obtained at www.ICGtesting.com
Printed in the USA
LVOW11s2204050516

486935LV00004B/192/P

4680040

9 780983 683117